RUNNING **CONTRA DICTION**

May each step bring you closer

Matt Padwick

RUNNING
CONTRA
DICTION

A NOVEL BY
MATT PADWICK

Published by Inner Temple Press
Castletownbere, West Cork, Ireland

inner.temple.press@gmail.com

See also
www.facebook.com/running.contradiction

ISBN: 978-0-9931840-0-0

ASPIRATION AND DEDICATION
May we dissolve all our inner conflicts
and thereby end civil disputes, foreign wars and
environmental degradation.

"Run only if you must.
If running is an imperative that comes from inside of
you...Otherwise heed the inner calling of your own
play...do what you do best and feel best at."
Dr George Sheehan

CONTENTS

1

THE END

1973: Late at night a young family and all they owned travelled west to Wales. The baby was sleeping as they crossed the old Severn Bridge. In those days there was only one.

◈

The young boy repeated the word quietly and to himself. Edward. Edward. Ed-ward. The word that was already so common to him, yet he had never really considered it. ED. WARD. It was a label for something he could not explain. How could that sound, those syllables, mean all that? And at the same time mean nothing?

◈

The clouds parted and a huge index finger pointed at him. No booming voice, no message, but that feeling of divine purpose didn't leave him. At the end of the Spiderman movie Uncle Ben says, "With power comes great responsibility." Ed felt all the responsibility and none of the power.

◈

Ed went to a church school but never went to church except on the big days. He spent his childhood family holidays in a caravan on a farm in the mountains of mid-Wales. It was like heaven to him. While there the family did go to church. Each Sunday.

After a week of no TV and poor radio reception it seemed like the natural thing to do. The church was on the side of a hill. Everything was on the side of a hill.

After the service the vicar would be waiting at the door. He would greet each person with something different. One Sunday, when he took Ed's hand, he said, "Go out into the world and be of good courage." He said it in a way that left Ed feeling courage was both necessary and possible.

◆

In secondary school there were two Edwards in the same class so they needed nicknames. One Edward was a prefect, got A's in exams, captained the rugby team and went on to join the Royal Marines on a scholarship programme. He was known as "Steady Eddie". Our Edward was "Scrambles", as in Scrambled Ed.

◆

Ed stood on a railway bridge in Scotland, sixty metres above the river. He didn't know how deep the water was, or what was downstream. He jumped anyway. What the fuck. It was not a death wish, but a way to feel alive.

"What was all that about?" The question was shallow and, as always, there was no space left for any kind of answer.

Since university Ed had been travelling, working seasons, moving on. He hung out with edgy people who jumped from one extreme sport to the next, only satisfied when poisoned by adrenalin, competing against the elements or each other or themselves. Especially themselves.

They were environmentally friendly and full of aggression. They drank too much and shouted a lot. They had enough money and had been to all the exotic places. As long as they kept moving there was no reason to enter the scary void – the real adventure that lurked inside themselves. Ed sensed this and wanted to stop but didn't know how, which screwed him up even more.

Between seasons and adventures he called on friends and stayed at his folks' place, but not for long; that was too close to the person he was running away from, the one he couldn't live with. During one of those home visits he called to a friend's house. They were heading into town for a pint. The friend was looking for his shoes. Ed waited at the bottom of the stairs.

To end the awkward silence Friend's Wife asked what he was doing these days. Ed talked for a minute, a mish-mash of past exploits and future options, to which she said,

"It's funny with you, you never seem to know if you are waving or drowning…" – Ed's friend was taking too long – "…on paper you should be waving, in practice I am not sure you are."

The first pint went down very quickly. He had several more before he was proud again. And he didn't stop there. They left after closing time. He rode alone on the last bus back to the village. He watched the bus rumble on and stood in the night on the side of the road. Walking from the stop he leant himself, and all that insecurity, on a gate, looking at the lights of the town below.

When he was a kid he could make out a skier, with long skis and bent knees, arms outstretched, and a big bobble hat. It had made the child dream.

Over the years the town had spilled out across the valley, an amorphous mess of violent orange. The skier must still be in there somewhere though.

The week before he had been sitting at a table surrounded by snow mountains drinking beer in the afternoon sun.

❖

Neil Young sang, *Old man take a look at my life, I'm a lot like you were…twenty-four and there's so much more . . .*

Ed was 24. That morning, soon after dawn, he and two others had ducked under a fence that said "Avalanche Risk". They traversed the slope until they were looking at the north face. They sat on the ridge just looking at it; if only you could bottle that feeling. In less than an hour they were back in the village with fist-pounds, hand-grabs and back-slaps all round. Now they were sitting at a table surrounded by snow mountains drinking beer in the afternoon sun, and shouting over Neil Young.

"What's next? "

"You mean whose round is it?"

"No, I mean what is next?"

Around this time Ed heard that Steady Eddie had lost a leg in Kurdistan. Steady Eddie had only one leg. The irony was too much.

❖

When he was in junior school, Ed's father helped him learn for a test. It was all a confusing mass of dates, long names and foreign places. So his dad gave him the context of the story, showed him how the facts fitted together; the dates and names and places flowed, there was a sequence. There was a sequence and it made sense. Someone needed to make sense of this. Pain hurt and so did fun. And where were the role models?

Utterly dislocated from any sense of meaning.

His options were running out.

He didn't like who he was.

And he didn't like what he didn't know.

And there didn't seem to be any escape.

And he couldn't escape that.

And there were consequences to feeling like this.

He made a pledge to himself. He would be thirty in six years. If he had still not found what he was looking for by then, he'd assume it wasn't out there and give up, join the flock and bleat about the state of the world, live in a house with a fence around it, put on weight and get old.

Six years.

2

Ireland...Meeting Streaky...Contra diction
Waking Up...Big One...Biggest One...Green Road

IRELAND

AUTUMN 2002. Sixteen days before his thirtieth birthday.
Three zero.

His granny was Irish. The Irish were Celts. There were
mountains and waves and no crowds. Binge drinking was celebrated, not criminalized. There were mid-season offers on the
ferry. Mr Blanco, his white 25-year-old VW Kamper van, had
started first time, just like the last time. He was good to go.

Ed's dis-ease became obvious while queueing for the boat.
The weather was calm, so it wasn't that, more the feeling that he
was leaving forever.

Waving or drowning? Screw you! My hand is up because I have a
question, okay. A question no-one can answer.

Recently he'd been having a recurring dream: he was in a
steep, wooded valley making slow and painful progress over fall-
en trees, brambles and briers. In the bottom of the valley were
the tracks, there was a train coming, moving in his direction, it
was the train he needed to get on, no idea where it was going,
it had blacked out windows. If you got on you couldn't get off.
That's all he knew. That was the deal.

Sitting in the queue for the ferry, wedged between two vehicles, he could not go forward, or back, and had no experience
of sitting still. He was about to be swallowed up by the ferry and

5

spat out the other side. He tried to comfort himself. He *was* on the move again, he *would* find what he was looking for.

❖

Ed was sitting on a dune at the western edge of western Europe, lost in destructive reverie. He had been there all day.

Over his shoulder was the village; the painted houses were a palette of colour at the foot of the barren rock mountain. Harder to see were the natural stone ruins from the copper mining days, the engine houses and stamping mills and the miners' homes.

The breeze moved clouds across the sun, and the shades and shadows shifted again and again over the water and headlands and islands. This day the sea had been every colour of blue and green. The tide had come and gone. After each tide the stream carved a new path back to mother.

He was sitting in the warm sand which glowed golden in the early evening. All this natural drama caused little more than a hiccup in the constant commentary in Ed's head. He helped himself to another handful of sand and gave it back again. And again. Repeatedly.

He'd walk up the beach. Down the beach. Then sit again and scoop some more. He mumbled some Bob Dylan.

How many seas must a white dove sail
before she sleeps in the sand?

He tipped the hood up over his head and lay back.

How many times must a man look up
Before he can see the sky?

He rolled his head to the left and heard the noise of the stream. He rolled his head to the right and felt the breeze on his face.

Help.

A few parents were somewhere between sitting and lying down, reading a book and wondering what was for dinner. Their children had brief swims in the chilly water and played in the sand. Not the kind you can make castles out of – too coarse and dry. You could be buried in it, but if you tried to take a breath it would pour into your lungs. It was that kind of sand.

Ed *did* notice the runner, the same one from the morning.

You can't make castles with it, walking on it was two-steps-forward-one-step-back, and yet this guy was gliding across the dune in a weightless way.

No-one else noticed the runner, they were all otherwise engaged, too busy with whatever was going on for them.

The runner looped around the children and their sand-mounds, crossed the stream, skipped over the boulders, barefoot without missing a beat, and disappeared up the road.

Ed remembered being on a river beach in Nepal sleeping under a raft. It's the middle of a half-moon night and he wakes up, can't say why, and looks out from under the raft and sees silhouettes moving over the expedition's kit. Still half-asleep he calls out before his feet are out of the sleeping bag which gives the thieves a head start. The bodies scatter, he chases the one with biggest looking bundle across the beach.

The thief lightens his load one item at a time until all he's carrying is Magnus's camera case. Ed is gaining on him as he reaches the beach-edge where a mountain stream cuts across the sand on its way to the river. The sand became pebbles, stones and sharp rocks. The thief runs on without hesitation, his bare feet of crocodile skin turning like a wheel under his body. Ed is stopped dead like he's hit a defence shield in a sci-fi movie. The thief gets away.

He hadn't thought about that again until today.

The sunset. Why does such beauty break your heart?

How could he know so much, and understand nothing?

He was too undone to even lift his head. He dug his right hand into the sand and watched it fall through his fingers.

Oh! This was his childhood nightmare, his "dream-job"! The

one that woke him up sweating. He had to count the grains of sand on the beach. It was impossible but Ed does not give up, Ed can be relied upon, Ed can do it. Except he couldn't. And can't. He would always try, try, try and fail, fail, fail before finally he woke up knotted in his blankets.

Everything was coming together in a really painful way. Or falling apart...

The deputy headmistress in secondary school had a mantra, "You've got no hope if you can't cope." And she always said it in such a high-strained tone. Whenever she addressed an individual, or the whole school, she would manage to work that one in. It always struck Ed as a strange thing to be saying to neurotic adolescents facing their next bout of exams.

He cheered himself with a favourite line from *Northern Exposure*, when Chris Stevens the radio jock says, "You have to lose your mind before you can find it." That was calming – there was hope, the possibility that it did not just keep getting worse.

The families were gone and the sun was set, he sat there still. Then he moved off to Mr Blanco, parked on the far side of the stream, and slid the door shut on the world.

A middle-aged man was walking his dog. "That's the life!" he said to himself. He had always dreamed of owning a camper van.

MEETING STREAKY

MORNING, and Ed was back at his spot with his head between his knees grabbing sand by the handful. Living your dream can be a difficult place to be if you discover it's not what you want. Where to from here? How can someone be so lucky, and so frustrated? Can't even generate sympathy for yourself. Too ashamed to complain to others.

He smoked a roll-up looking at the ocean, seeing nothing.

Someone was coming. He wiped his nose with one sleeve and his eyes with the other.

"You're lucky with the weather." It was the runner.

" I 'er yeah…"

" Streaky," he said, holding out a hand. Streaky had grey hair and lines but the posture and being of a younger man. His skin was not overcooked and leathery like the local fishermen, but the effortless brown of beach holidays.

He had somehow got inside Ed's antisocial vibe and was already sitting down. They say that you'll tell a stranger things you wouldn't tell a friend. Ed started with last night's sunset which somehow became the bridge in Scotland, and the avalanche in Austria and the waterfall in Nepal.

Streaky just chuckled, but with the right vibration, not against Ed. "Like an accident *wanting* to happen you are so. One foot in the grave, the other on a banana skin."

Gannets were diving in the morning sun; Streaky paused, he gave them their moment. "An avalanche…all that violence, craziness and destruction, but actually it is nature's way of restoring harmony, balancing out an over-steep, unstable situation."

Another pause.

"Instead of acting out, chasing your tail, maybe you could try staying still. It could save a lot of time, money and energy. And maybe even a premature death."

A large dog pounded by them with its tongue hanging out.

"Which, by the way, is the sadness of the sunset. A reminder of the transient nature of everything. There is no pause button. Having a camera helps. You can pretend it's saved. You have *captured* it. But that's the same as saying you've been someplace when actually you only found it on a map."

The dog ran back with a ball and a knot of seaweed wedged in its jaws.

"Cloudy days are less of a challenge. No dramatic sunsets.

They come and go, it's easier not to notice, not to care. Much easier is to live a lifetime of cloudy days and one day drop dead none-the-wiser."

Ed was still scooping sand, but he was listening.

"Did you ever read any William Blake?"

To see a world in a grain of sand
And a heaven in a wild flower
Hold infinity in the palm of your hand
And eternity in an hour.

"A world in a grain of sand…there, now, you are holding the story of the mountain and the mines in your hand. Maybe not in the way Blake intended, but this sand is a portal to another world. Less than two hundred years ago this sand was bedrock in the heart of that mountain. Working sometimes half a mile underground, using gunpowder and pick axes, the miners brought it to the surface where it was crushed and stamped using steam engines. The spoil was flushed into the stream and, year-after-year washed down here. This beach is made of everything they didn't need. Today's children are making castles with the blood, sweat and tears of the miners and their families."

CONTRA DICTION

STREAKY stretched his legs out straight in front of him, leaned forward until his face was just about on his knees then, very slowly, returned to an upright position, crossing his legs once more.

" What I realised was, in my own life there was a fundamental contradiction. I want to be happy. And I want to avoid suffering. But my actions do not support this aspiration. And when

I looked around, just about everyone else was stuck in the same jam.

"That, right there, is the running contradiction, the cycle of frustration we find ourselves locked into. While looking for happiness we attract suffering. Our misguided efforts just lead to more frustration. What I realised was – stop your digging for a minute – it's like this, take a few grains of this sand between your thumb and fingers, feel the sand between your thumb and forefinger. We are looking for oil by the way. Now squeeze. Press! Give it all you've got...

"What happens? Nothing! It's hopeless.

"No matter how hard we try we will never get oil from these grains of sand. No matter how good our intention, or how much effort we apply, regardless of the angle we put on it, or the vices we employ, we will not get oil from these grains of sand.

"All we discover is a new layer of frustration, dissatisfaction, tension, stress, perhaps a node of anger or a pocket of aggression.

"It's obvious. So what's my point?

"First, *happy* is a big word. We need to define it for ourselves. If you want to find something the first step is to know what you are looking for, no? What does *happy* mean to you? Do you want to be very rich, or very famous, or very powerful, or very successful? They are all very different. Or maybe you just want a little of each of the above, enough to be joyful and content?

"Second, we look for happiness in all the places that it will never be, never has been, is not. Which is outside of ourselves. Happiness does not, cannot, exist outside of ourselves.

Happiness that is dependant upon the perfect arrangement of a set of outer circumstances is difficult to achieve and impossible to preserve because everything is always changing, usually in a way we can't control. But that does not stop us trying. It's all very strained. And unstable. Even when things do come together in a 'happy way' we are so busy trying to keep it that way we forget to enjoy it. Can you see how vulnerable that makes us? It's so effort-full and so futile. That's why I say while we are looking for happiness we attract suffering. My kind of happiness is simple, is contentment. It's subjective, a feeling inside of me, not a set of circumstances. It makes sense doesn't it? If happiness was an object or place or person we would be able to buy it. And it would come with a guarantee.

"Back to oil. The modern world seems convinced that we need oil to make us happy. The Americans invaded Iraq looking for oil, to make themselves happy. It was another example of mankind looking in the wrong place in the wrong way for happiness, and being surprised when it eludes them. Again. Another example of mankind creating a present hell in order to reach a future heaven – even though the future never arrives."

Ed was getting some of this. He travelled the world and drove a Vee-Dub, wore polyester and used a computer. He could see the oil, but he didn't feel the happiness…and oil was just an example of a greater contradiction.

Streaky wasn't finished. "Do you ever go running?"

Ed had not said anything for a while, he just wanted to sit quietly and think about things one at a time.

"Me, running? Eh, only if I am late for something. Or I am being chased? Maybe I am too lazy. My knees are a bit wrecked from…"

"Lazy? It's not a question of being lazy. It's dull. Don't get me wrong, there can be magic in the midst of any activity, but it doesn't get much purer than perfectly putting one foot in front of the other."

Ed laughed a good laugh and waited for Streaky to join him. Streaky didn't laugh.

". . . and people don't get injured because they are running, but the way they are running. I run natural style, it works with or without shoes. When I run natural style, my mind has to give its full attention to my body. Aimless free-wheeling is just not an option. Or you could say, running natural style, the body *catches* the mind, reins in the mind, brings the mind home to the present action and the present moment. For as long as we run our body and mind are in union, in the present moment. We are 'in the zone' or 'flowing' and we like it. And we want to experience that naturalness in other areas of our life."

❖

Streaky was distracted for a few moments by a child flying a kite. Turning back to Ed, he said, "I am not staying, have some unfinished business to attend to. There is a low in the Atlantic that will be with us tomorrow. The summer is over. You see that shed on the headland – there is only one – that's my place. The key is under the frog, you can park your van inside there, the living room is down the steps, there's no electricity but the wood stove heats the water and the rads. And go running. It'll ease some of that intensity out of you. And run barefoot. Start on the old Green Road up to the lighthouse. Take it slow. In the beginning walk more. Remember a long stride is a sign of pride, which anybody will tell you is followed by a fall. So take it easy…With the running and with all this other stuff, the main thing is, take your time. You'll get there. Isaac Newton was fierce clever and he said, *What we know is a drop, what we don't know is an ocean.* If you spend some time here I think you'll find this beach has got all the metaphors and similes you'll ever need. And remember – what feels like a nervous break-down may just be a nervous break-through." He stood up and took off across the dune.

WAKING UP

"WHERE the hell am I?" he said to himself, rubbing his eyes and looking out of the van windows at the natural stone walls.

13

Ed had slept long into the next day.

Do you get that ever? A few days and nights without sleep that felt like a lifetime? Then the sleep comes, which is so deep it could be the final sleep, and returning from that is like falling back to earth.

A gust of wind slammed against the barn door and it heaved in its runners and against the locks. "There is a low in the Atlantic that will be with us tomorrow. The summer is over," he repeated to himself as he put the pieces together. This was the storm. The guy from the beach, Streaky, this was his place.

He climbed out of the sleeping bag, slid open the side door and stepped out of the van. In front of him was a work bench with some tools hanging above it. There was enough room to walk around the van. At the other side of the van firewood was stacked neatly along the length of the wall. Two clear panels in the corrugated roof provided some natural light and there was a small window in the front wall, facing the ocean. He looked through that. The shed was right over the water, just a short, very steep, grassy slope and the ocean boiling beneath him.

A suddenly strong gust of wind blew a bucketful of water at the window. Ed recoiled. He was still waking up.

At the back of the shed, facing the mountain, was the heavy sliding door. He unbolted the Judas gate and went to step out. The little door was ripped from his grasp. A black thing flew across his vision, from left to right, and out of sight. Its wings were at an awkward angle and it appeared to be looking over its shoulder. Had he just seen a hooded crow being blown backwards up the hill?

It was an uncommon wind; it hissed and roared and lambasted the land, cursing every obstacle in its path. He levered himself back inside and bolted the door closed. It rattled back at him.

"The living room is down the steps," he repeated to himself, tapping the concrete floor with his left foot. Down the steps?

14

Then he saw the wooden boards. Mr Blanco was parked over a vehicle inspection pit, that would be "steps".

He took Mr Blanco out of gear and pushed him forward so the front bumper kissed the front wall and went to the rear again, lifted the first board set in the concrete floor which revealed a step, removed another board, more steps, until he was standing under his van facing a glass-panelled wooden door.

Ed opened the door and three paces in front of him was the back door of a wooden cabin with a grass sod roof.

"This Streaky is unusual alright…"

Invisible from the road, difficult to see even through the sea-facing window of the stone shed just above it, this cabin was built right on the edge of the steep grassy slope, which became the cliff, which plunged into the sea.

"Holy shit!"

Ed was standing in the cabin. There was one large round window, as tall as he was, facing the ocean, a giant peep-hole on the world.

Standing in the middle of the floor was a tree trunk holding up the roof.

There were two roof windows, so even on an overcast day like this natural light bathed the floor. Along the back wall was a range-style cooking stove, with a few pots and pans and plates and crockery under a sink. He turned the tap, clean looking water came out.

He looked out of the big round window at the sky; the ocean was some way below.

He opened the door on the left hand wall. A toilet, more like a throne, standing smack in the middle of a small bathroom, with a porthole overlooking the ocean. Behind it a sink and a shower.

Coming back into the living space he saw the futon and the bookshelves. And the candle surrounded by shells on the small table in front of the big round window.

"There's no electricity but the wood stove heats the rads…"

He had tea bags in Mr B. He would light the stove, warm the place up, take a shower. But first he would pinch himself.

BIG ONE

A MUG of steaming tea rested in the arc of his cupped hands. To be drinking black tea without complaint, with relish even, must mean he was having an adventure.

Black tea, tea without milk, without even powdered milk, meant something was not quite right. Like the time he was sitting on a remote river-beach in Nepal with three people who were hating him.

❖

They were five hours downstream of unremitting, violently exciting, treacherously exhausting, adrenalin-pumping white-water kayaking. They were in a gorge, there was only one way out. Three more days to go and, at the end, "The Big One".

They all wished they were back in Kathmandu.

The night before they had been upstairs in The Third Eye, a favourite haunt for pseudo-locals in the heart of the tourist section of Kathmandu.

They knew if they were going to attempt this river descent they needed as much information as they could get. All they had so far was a map. A piece of paper with a blue line on it. They needed to speak to people who had been there, seen it and done it.

Only two people had ever run this river before. They were known as The Whitewater Gurus. Brian was trembling with excitement – he'd arranged a meet.

"Don't worry, it's a bargain," bragged Brian, who was the

16

unofficial expedition leader. "We have to buy them a meal and their beers. And one of them doesn't even drink!"

❖

"Watch out for the big one right at the end," said the first Guru. He was sober and kind-of gleaming, a well-groomed, six-foot-tall perfect physical specimen with a constant smile. And crow's-feet around his eyes which said *sunshine and wisdom*.

The Gleaming Guru didn't drink; the other one did. The second Guru looked like he'd been in a cave for 700 years waiting for Robert the Bruce to return – he was a mass of hair and fore-arms. He drank beer from the bottle, straining it through his beard.

"Your round, laddee, shake a leg!" said The Caveman Guru

"But you..."

"I gots two hands, I needs two beers. And we'll take a wee dram too."

It was like sitting in a taxi, in a traffic jam, the meter spinning.

It was close to midnight and The Gurus wouldn't even talk about the river until now. Every time Brian brought the subject back to The Forbidden River, each time The Caveman Guru would say to The Gleaming Guru, "Do nay say nuthin'. They'us nay able for it. Look at 'em. They'us mammies'll miss 'em."

But finally The Gleaming Guru relented.

"Thanks for the food, and you've done a reasonable job of quenching Dougie's thirst, so about this river...the first day is some good value play-boating, the second and third are mellow. But on the fourth day, at the end, it's big. You'll hear it long before you see it. It's on a tight bend. You'll definitely want to get out and inspect from the bank but the eddy above is only big enough for one, maybe two, kayaks...he looked along the line of four protegés barely out of kayak kindergarten..."so there'll not be space for all of you."

The Gleaming Guru was only half right. Brian and Rob

17

were whitewater stars of their generation, perhaps even The Gurus of the future. They would make the eddy for sure. Ed and Seamus were a liability and would have been concerned to hear this, if they'd heard it. But the team was distracted again, this time by some Scandinavian trekkers.

The Gleaming Guru also gave them a tourist map and circled the Kathmandu bus station on it.

"The bus goes from there…oh, and at the put-in, get on the river as quick as possible. There's a village official who, if he sees you in time, will sting you for $30 each for an extra permit you don't need." They got up to leave. "And watch out for that Big One."

The Caveman Guru looked at them. "Keep yer weed dry. Ye'll be glad ye deed."

The crowd parted as the two Gurus made their way to the door. They had their photo on the Temple Bar's "Himalayan Wall of Fame".

The boys watched them leave.

It was quiet except for the booming music and everyone else in the bar shouting at each other. Seamus spoke first. "I don't know about this, me and the Robmeister have only just arrived, maybe we should hang around, acclimatise, meet some ladies."

"That's just great," said Rob looking at the place in his wallet where all the crisp rupee notes used to be. " That cost us a fortune. I only got here this morning and I could have told you how to find the bloody bus station."

Brian and Ed were half-way through a river-guiding season; their boss was in India renewing his passport, this was their opportunity for a trip.

Still Ed had doubts. "I missed some of it but that Big One sounded pretty big. Did he say *You'll be glad you did* or *You'll be glad you're dead?*"

Ed looked at his beer, and at the Scandinavian trekkers.

"Mmm... maybe Seamus is right. Town is good right now."

Guiding an inflatable raft down Himalayan glacier-melt rivers swollen by the monsoon rain demanded a lot of skill and understanding, especially when the crews were globe-trotting novices – some of whom couldn't swim or were even afraid of water or suffering from debilitating stomach upsets. Or all of the above.

Ed was a raft-guide on paper; in practice he had a lot to learn. In his first season he had repeatedly, unwittingly, flipped his raft sending his crew swimming down the river several times a day. Brian was a good friend on the river, teaching and advising Ed in quiet moments, never in front of the raft crews. And Brian always led the river trips and was always downstream, so all Ed's casualties got washed towards him. Brian would fish them out and collect stray paddles and other floating debris, and was so pumped with the adrenalin and excitement of it all everyone thought it must just be part of the show. In the evening around the campfire the girls dripped off him, their dreams condensing under the stars.

Ed's raft guiding had improved but he was still more comfortable sitting on a bar stool.

"Lads, Lads!" called Brian, eventually getting their attention. Brian was fully focused on the kayak trip, a lot more concerned with his trajectory to Guru status than getting an erection. He puffed his pectorals and rubbed his crotch. "Lads, this would be the second descent ever of a Himalayan river."

Now Brian had a point there, they might even get their photo on the Wall of Fame. "When the word gets round you won't need to meet the ladies, Seamus, they'll be meeting you."

Duties were delegated: kit, food, permits and bus tickets. After detailing the plan, followed by questions and visits to the bar and toilet, Brian made them take it in turns to repeat it back. Each of them needed help, but between them they had it.

Then Ed saw Charlotte.

He looked round to warn Brian. Brian was already gone.

❖

Ed had always had enough money to live comfortably, but in Nepal he lived like a king. After some days out rafting or trekking, returning to Kathmandu was like arriving in Shangri-La – free-wheeling his bike into town from the guides' house, in the glare of the morning sun, swerving through the swarm of busy bees gathering their subsistence wage, sinking into the comfort of a barber's chair. The barber jokes about cutting the dreadlocks before giving him a hot shave and a very casual head massage; then to a breakfast café: will it be a hotel restaurant, or a rooftop, or a garden?

He could order anything off the menu, and would stay there reading a book or listening to bootleg tapes on his Walkman for as long as he wanted, or until someone he knew rocked up and suggested they go somewhere for lunch.

That was the hang-over morning schedule. But he never really had been able to binge-drink for more than two nights in a row. So some mornings he woke up fresh. Restless. He might run through the streets of Thamel, dodging cows in the early morning mist, and out to the Monkey Temple, up the hundreds of steps before falling in line with the devotees walking clock-wise around the bright white stupa, getting his breath back under the painted eyes of the Buddha. Swayambhunath, also known as the Monkey Temple, was one of the oldest and most sacred sites in the Kathmandu Valley. On that crowded hill-top, everyone was looking for meaning in life but Ed had already crossed religion off the list of options, so he ran down the far side of the mountain past monasteries and the residences of eminent lamas.

This was just to relax his body and to clear his head; now he could shower and enjoy his breakfast.

Ed had a left-field charm and mystic mentality that suited Kathmandu. But his left-field charm and mysticism expired after about five beers, so while everyone else got relaxed and happy, Ed hatched into a left-wing ensorcelled miscreant. But by that time the party was under way…

Brian's body was his temple. And he welcomed worshippers of all female denominations. Once the party was started he would decide which fair maiden was going to market and expertly and easily separate her from the flock. When people went to Kathmandu they were ready for something magical to happen. When a girl looked into Brian's eyes they knew it was true.

With clear speech, fresh breath, eye-lids aflutter and muscles quietly rippling under an unstained T-shirt, he introduced himself. "Brian, Brian Hill. My friends call me Brill."

She could see most of what she wanted to know about Brill but there were some obvious gaps. "Why don't you drink?" she might ask.

Brill liked this one, especially if Ed had drunk six or more beers, was in view and in mid-antic-ulation. "Because I have to look after him," he would say, nodding in Ed's direction.

She can't believe it. Her dream has come true! She's found a sensitive, caring man. With muscles. She may fan herself a little before following Brill's gaze across the room.

Ed is wearing a long-sleeve rainbow shirt and board shorts, standing on a table, smoking a roll-up he's holding between his toes. He exhales, and does a little hop to keep balanced.

"Okay, okay," he shouts, "I am saying I can climb down under this table and up the other side without touching the floor. And you say I can't. Put you money where your…"

He tumbles from the table into a group of German mountaineers.

The girl panics. "But you don't have to look after him tonight, do you?" she asks.

Brian watches Ed for a moment longer. The Germans are just pushing him around and shouting; it's not like he'd landed on Israelis.

"No, not tonight."

Bingo!

Is that her thinking Bingo*! Or is it him? Both of course. This is destiny.*

Sometimes Ed resented being a pawn in Brill's sex traffic. He even considered being more amenable himself, calming down and being a bit more presentable, but then something would happen that would make him realise he was lucky *not* to be the lucky one.

◈

When they were not on the river or leading treks, and when the boss was in town, the guides spent the day in the office selling trips to tourists.

One morning Ed and Brian were doing their office duty when Bridget appeared at the door in floods of tears. It turns out Brill had given one of his "free spirit" speeches over breakfast, and Bridget was digesting the fact that the wedding she had been imagining for the past two days was off.

Brill suggested they go somewhere for coffee and clarification.

Thirty minutes later Ed was across the table from an adventurous couple who were about to book a rafting trip.

Brill stole in the door. "I'm not here!" he hissed over the heads of the couple, and disappeared into the back office.

"So, any more questions?" Ed said to his clients.

"Arghhhh!.. Where is heeeee?" screamed Bridget falling through the door, pulling at her hair and a good bit crazier looking than before.

"He, er, is having coffee with you," said Ed.

Ed had just lied. Everyone knew it. Including the highly distressed woman who was blocking the exit. Bridget took a big inhale. Time stood still. Ed lowered in his chair, making sure the adventurous couple were between him and her.

Time still hadn't moved. It was real High Noon. Fingers on triggers.

There was a loud crash from the back office – probably Brian trying to escape through the bars on the window. Bridget's head twitched in that direction.

"He's in there, isn't he?" she said to herself in a man's voice, storming across the room.

"We'll come back later," said the adventurous couple.

"Me too," said Ed, hopping the desk.

But there was no-one quite like Charlotte.

❖

On a day when Ed was holding the office, Charlotte appeared at the door wearing a floral print dress, wool socks and worn-out walking boots. She was asking for directions. Ed went back out onto the street with her to point the way, but they ended up getting chai from a street vendor and sitting on a step in the sun.

Charlotte was easily less than thirty but somehow she was already an award-winning architect who worked half-the-year in the city of her choice and spent the other six months travelling. There was an exhibition of her art in Switzerland and she was here to meet an American film crew who were making a documentary about her.

She walked everywhere. China, Burma and Vietnam. She travelled alone and light, everything was in the satchel over her shoulder. This time she was arriving overland from Tibet. In between villages she had spent freezing nights sheltering in hollows without even a sleeping bag.

But none of that was the most impressive thing about her. What was *really* impressive about her was, she was hot looking! And easy to listen to, and be with.

Charlotte wasn't the cardboard cut-out style of beauty. There was no way she could play a boy-part in a Shakespeare production. Or hide behind a pencil.

"There's a party tonight at the Embassy. Would you like to come?" Ed said all that sober and without stuttering or getting the words in the wrong order. They said Kathmandu was where magic happened. It was true!

Ed had a date. This was fate. Even the world was rhyming.

Charlotte had washed her dress and invested in a pair of flip-flops. She already knew her way around the city so called by to pick Ed up and they dropped in to a few bars on the way. Ed's left-field charm and mystic mentality were serving him well.

When they arrived at the party, the music was thumping – The Doors, LA Woman – and there were hundreds of tins of chilled European beer in the middle of the garden perfectly stacked in a pyramid that was as tall as Ed. Civilisation indeed. It was beautiful.

He turned to elicit some professional appreciation from his architect-artist date but Charlotte was not there. She was on the terrace. She was being Brilled.

Ed was gutted. He hadn't opened a tin in a while. He really liked the sound.

A few tins later, Ed was wearing the host's pink dressing gown. He had just won the breath-hold competition in the frog-pond. In fact if someone had not fished him out he might still have been in there.

"That water is rancid. What was he doing in the pond anyway?"

Charlotte and Brill were having a good time. They left together.

The pyramid was almost finished. But not quite.

❖

Charlotte rented a downtown rooftop apartment close to where she was filming. Brian moved out of the guides' house. He moved in with her.

This had never happened before. It was *so* against the un-written Guide's Code of Non-Ethics that no-one knew how to respond.

So they didn't.

It was ten whole days later before they saw Brian again when he moved back to the guides' house with his tail back between his legs.

No-one knew how to respond to that either. So they didn't.

But Brian needed to confide, and he shared a room with Ed, so Ed heard how he'd written Charlotte a letter about being a free spirit, and she hadn't taken it so well.

That was last week; he had been held captive for three days.

"Captive? How?"

"I don't know. She is much cleverer than me. When someone that intelligent goes crazy it's scary."

◈

Very late that same night. "It's not her," said Brian, sure that Ed had also been woken by the noise. "It can't be, she doesn't know where I live."

It sounded like the night watchman had tried to detain someone at the gate. There was some crashing. Now it was silent again. Except for the usual deafening chorus of barking dogs.

The front door of the house opened. And slammed shut. There were footsteps on the stone stairs. Ed pretended he was asleep.

He was sure it was her. She did know where Brian lived. The same place as Ed. She had called in that first night in her freshly pressed floral print dress and flip-flops on the way to the party.

"Even if it is her, she doesn't know which room I am in," said the frightened voice in the next bed. Mmmm. There were four bedrooms. The other guides were all out on the rivers or trekking, and their rooms were empty. She would probably be able to work it out.

She opened the first door. Arun and Samir were on the Trisuli. The second door. Claudia was at Everest Base Camp, and Jay was on the Sun Kosi.

The third. Sam and Raj were on their way back from Pokhara.

Their door must be next.

Ed was interested to note that his visualisation had Charlotte carrying a cricket bat.

"Oh shit," thought Ed. "How will she know which bed has Brian in it?…Because she is clever, that's how! One side of the room is a mess, the other side of the room is organised with an alarm clock on the table and dumbbell weights on the floor."

He was so relieved he nearly farted.

Their door opened.

He covered the soft parts of his body. His whole body felt soft.

Nothing. For a few moments nothing. Then there was a crash.

A loud crash like the sound of a lump of timber hitting the wardrobe. She did have a cricket bat!

Another crash. And a third. This time with the splintering of wood.

Then a very calm voice said, "Brill, honey, I know you are not asleep."

Now with an icy edge, "Show your face…c'mon, be the man." No response. There was a pause. A really long one.

There was a faint scratching noise. The bedroom door slammed. Maybe she had released a venomous spider in the room, or a snake.

The house front door slammed.

No noise at the gate. The watchman must still be unconscious or on his way to hospital.

"Oh shit. Ah no! Ah Christ! No way!"

Ed peeked out from under the covers. Brian was sitting up in the bed across the room, shining a torch at the end of his bed. Smart, much too risky to put the light on. Oh. It was his cherrywood composite custom rafting paddle, handmade by Randy Finkelman, Canada's finest paddle-craftsman, personally presented to him for leading a college expedition to the Tundra. It was in two pieces. She'd broken it over the end of his bed.

Next to it was a piece of paper.

Brian read it under his breath, but he was breathing quite hard so Ed could hear,

"I could have killed you in your bed.

Would have been too easy.

It's not over.

See you tomorrow.

Charlotte

X"

Without warning Brian shone the torch at Ed who was blinded and shocked.

"Er, sorry about the paddle."

He put the covers back over his head so it was clear he had no more to offer. Some friend.

That was the night before the meeting with The Gurus.

Brill needed to skip town for a while.

❖

The morning after meeting The Gurus, the lads were on the bus.

Actually on the bus. Riding on the roof among the sacks of wool, caged chickens and their kayaks.

They had started off sitting with all the people and uncaged chickens inside the bus but the wooden seats, loosely bolted to the rusty floor, were too uncomfortable.

Hair was important. Especially when surfing the roof of a bus travelling into the foothills of the Himalayas. Ed's curls were getting pretty big. Definitely moving in the breeze. Dreads were forming. Any minute now his hair would "drop" and he would look the part.

Brian was dishevelled in a designer kind of way. Occasionally, unnecessarily, he moved his fringe out of his eyes.

Seamus was next in line, unshaven and unkempt. He'd recently bought himself out of the Royal Navy. He wouldn't say why.

Rob had the shortest hair. He was on the sick from his job as a fitter at a power station in Leeds. It wasn't obvious how he was sick. Another secret.

"This river could have a story to it," said Seamus prophetically, rubbing his chin. They were all thinking it. It was a small miracle they'd got this far.

That morning had been quite unusual. Usually Brian switched off his alarm before it had a chance to wake Ed. And usually Brian didn't snore. Or smell.

This morning Brian snored on through his alarm, and Ed had to get up to switch it off. Which is what woke Seamus up. That was kind. With Charlotte still on the prowl, Brian offers his bed to a friend.

Ed and Seamus got on bicycles and free-wheeled into town, picking a breakfast cafe at random. Brian and Rob were already inside.

"Wow! I'm surprised you two remembered we were meeting here," said Rob through a mouthful of eggs.

"Yeah, okay, um, sorry we're late."

"You're twenty minutes early."

"Okay. Sorry."

"Do you remember the plan?"

"Sure."

"Yep."

"Right, the bus leaves at 10am."

At 10.07am Ed arrived. The driver was revving the bus, Brian was standing in front of the bus in crucifix posture, preventing it moving off. Rob was on the roof, strapping the kayaks on. The bus rocked forward two yards and back one. It belched dark smoke like a sick dragon staggering backwards about to sit on Brian.

"I'm late cos they took ages over the bus tickets," shouted Ed

"You were permits. Rob already got the bus tickets."

"Ah, okay, I remembered the food though."

Next, Seamus came running round the corner waving a fist full of bus tickets.

❖

Later that day, on the roof of the bus, riding these dusty roads cut into the valley wall, swerving the other vehicles, and animals, pedestrians and rockfalls...this was the first chance they had to take a quiet moment to reflect on what they were doing.

"I think this river could have a story to it. The put-in can't be that far now, we'll probably start winding down to the valley floor soon," said Seamus. Moments later the bus went up on two wheels rounding a bend, gravity straining to keep the vehicle and its occupants on the road; the lads had a spectacular view of the river, bright sunlight glaring off the surface of the foaming water a long way below.

The bus sped on up the valley towards the Tibet border. The river was coming up to meet the road. Ominous.

Twenty three hours after leaving Kathmandu the bus stopped on a bridge and sounded the horn. This would let the villagers know it had arrived, and was ready to leave already.

Crap! It would also wake up the village official that The Gurus had warned them about. In Nepal you could live like a king for a week on $30. The adrenalin began to flow as they threw the kayaks off the roof and scrambled down to the river, each one surrounded by children dressed in rags wanting to help.

"What is your name? Where is your country? This mine?"

Ed rammed any remaining belongings into the back of the kayak.

"Everybody ready!" shouted Seamus. He was never happier than when evading authority.

"Yep," shouted Ed, even though he wasn't. No wonder people robbed banks if this is what it felt like.

"Yep. Ready!" That was Rob.

"Brian! Are you ready?"

No answer.

"He's gone already. See you at the first break-out."

Ed sat in, sealed his deck, wiped his brow, clipped his helmet, gripped his paddle and signalled to the kids they could push. The moment the nose of the kayak hit the current it was spun downstream. An icy wave thumped his chest and took his breath away.

A child on the bank was wearing his sunglasses and another one had Rob's cap on. The morning light glared off the white water. Three silhouettes went under the road bridge in front of him. The last road they would see for four days.

Ed passed under the bridge too. He passed Brian who was parked up in an eddy. Brian smiled and winked. Then he passed Rob and Seamus, each sitting pretty in a quiet eddy.

On a road it is called a lay-by. On a river it is an eddy or break-out. On a narrow, steep, twisting river the eddies are small and rare.

In front of Ed the horizon was empty. That meant one thing – he was going down. Ideally one would stop, get out, take a look – but there was no place for him to pull in;.he would have to run it blind, like speeding round a corner not knowing what he would find. Except the corner was vertical and gravity was there to help.

Oh Mercy! It was just a ten-foot drop with a big plunge pool and a small eddy where he could pull over and hyperventilate for a while. He held his paddle vertically above his head so the others would know it was safe to follow.

It was their turn to look gripped as they were swept passed him.

◆

Five hours later they were sitting on a little river beach, the first they had seen all day. They would camp there. The river echoed noisily off the canyon walls. The sun rarely touched the ground this close to the centre of the earth.

The Gurus had called the first day the "play boating" section – but the lads were on their limit, and they couldn't be sure it was finished. They were up a creek, and there was only one way out. Three more days to go and, at the end, the "Big One".

They all kind of wished they were back in Kathmandu. Seamus wished it the most. How come he was sitting on a little patch of sand in the heart of the Himalayas with *one* headache, *two* sprained ankles, and *three* tormentors?

In amongst the waterfalls, pour-overs, strainers and grave-stones, Seamus, taking his turn to lead the group, had gone over an innocuous looking drop and landed on a rock which brought him to a sudden halt. All the impact was absorbed through his legs, compressing his ankles on the footrest. Immediately he was capsized and swept downstream by tonnes of glacier-melt water rushing down to the Indian plains. He continued round the next blind bend upside down, managing to roll himself upright on the third attempt.

Walking was difficult so Seamus had crawled on to beach. His helmet was on at a bit of an angle. Or was it his head? His pride was dented. He wanted to go to the toilet so he dug a hole and did it where he was.

Ed announced the expedition menu.

31

"We have teabags, honey, muesli and milk. Except I just looked and the ants are already at the honey."

"All we've got to eat for four days is muesli?"

"You said you liked muesli."

"I didn't say I *only* like muesli."

Everyone was a bit tetchy. Put some grub in them and they'll cheer up, thought Ed.

Anything they brought had to be carried in the kayaks with them. In the bar in Kathmandu (was it only two nights ago?), to save on space and weight wherever possible, they had decided not to pack their state-of-the-art camping stoves because there would be plenty of driftwood. Usually there would be driftwood. But the river was high, there was hardly any driftwood, and the few scraps they found were wet or green.

In the circumstances Ed's muesli plan was quite a good option.

"You don't have to cook muesli, we don't need a fire. And while we can't boil the river water, we all have some clean water left in our bottles, we can have muesli for supper."

Ed flicked the sand out of his tin mug and wiped his spoon on his sandy shirt, three-quarter filled the mug with muesli, spooned in some milk powder for a nice creamy taste, then carefully poured some of his precious clean water on top. It still looked so dry. He was ready for a good feed. Salivating, he emptied the rest of the water on top.

Everybody did the same. And began stirring and mixing.

"You prick!"

"You asshole!"

"Shit-for-brains!"

"Sorry lads." Ed had packed flour instead of milk powder.

Two hours later they had warmed some water on a sorry little campfire and made the saddest cup of tea in the history of mankind.

Seamus had already consumed the expedition's supply of pain-killers and was experiencing side-effects. This was their chance. They moved the toilet paper out of reach, and he wasn't allowed it back until he confessed.

"I don't believe it. You bastards! Because I don't like loud bangs okay! I bought myself out of the Navy because I don't like loud bangs. Now give me back the bog roll."

Being stuck in a shit storm can really bring a bunch of lads together. Either that or cannibalism. Ed wanted to go for a long walk but their beach was only a few paces long. He sat on a rock which felt more like a naughty stone.

"Anyway Rob," said Brian, "what about you? How come you are not fit for work?"

Rob pressed his lips together and looked at them one at a time. He was not sure he could trust these three guys. That said, two of them might not make it out of this alive, and he was in a lonely gorge in the heart of Asia, seven thousand kilometres away from his supervisor. It was probably safe to say.

"I've got a bad back."

"Jesus Christ!" they hissed back at him.

"What? It's nearly better now."

It was a very long evening. Sleep, when it came, was a blessed relief.

Come morning they strained their necks looking up at a clear blue sky. It was like looking up out of a toilet bowl. Surveying the sparse accumulation of green twiglets and dew-soaked toilet paper they gave up on the idea of a fire. Maybe if they just got straight on the river they could turn this four-day expedition into three days, or even two.

They got on the river, and around the first bend it went calm and silent. The valley sides opened out. Just like that.

The action of the previous day contrasted with this easy-going free-floating river journey. In any other circumstances it would have been a pleasant adventure through nature. This day it was a grind.

Brian and Rob set the pace because they were stronger. Perhaps also because they knew the eddy above The Big One was only big enough for two. Occasionally Ed dropped back to keep an uncomfortable Seamus company, but mostly was somewhere in between.

The day before they couldn't spit for fear. Today they couldn't spit because there was no spit to spare. The commotion in their minds and bowels was compensating for the calm river. They could all shit through the eye of a needle: perhaps it was giardiasis, perhaps dehydration. Probably a combination. And anxiety. After all, there was still The Big One.

That night they found a nice beach, but there was nothing to do. Except light a fire and boil enough water for a cup of tea each. There was a bit more wood and it wasn't so green, but it still took two hours. Then there was nothing to do again.

If they were somewhere else they could talk about a passion they had in common – like white-water kayaking – and their plans to run some unknown rivers in exotic parts of the world. Instead they talked about nutritious food, chilled beer and a comfortable, dry, warm bed.

❖

On the morning of the next day, Day Three, their river joined the Sun Kosi, which was one of the rivers Brian and Ed rafted often so they knew it well, each rapid, each flat section…all the way down to the town, and the road, at the start of the Indian plains.

"Wait. WAIT! If we are here – and that is there – then where is The Big One?

"The bastards! We've been waiting for something that doesn't exist. All that mental torment and nervy sphincter activity for nothing."

34

Brian and Rob were genuinely disappointed.

Seamus cut a sorrowful figure, like the badly injured person in a plane-crash movie, the one that survivors carry on the march to salvation because it's a moral obligation, not because they think he will make it or is even worth saving.

"There'll be tea at One Tree Village, which is about an hour," said Ed without a hint of regret that they would not be able to test their mettle against The Big One.

One Tree Village was a village in the sense that there was a collection of houses but it was still a day's walk from a tarred road.

"Oh yeah," continued Ed, positively carried away, "they always only have a lot of one thing for sale there. It must be whatever falls out the back of a porter's carry-basket. Once it was chickens. Last time it was those small sweet bananas. I must have had a whole bunch, maybe twelve. That night I had the maddest dreams – could even have been hallucinating."

Hallucinations sounded quite appealing to all of them. They tucked in their chins and paddled on.

In One Tree Village Ed was sitting on a rock under the one big tree in the village. He knew where he was. He wasn't lost any more. He could find himself on a map. If he had one.

It was a supremely comforting feeling. *You are going to be All Right.*

In order to feel All Right like this it is necessary to have been thoroughly lost, or to have been properly *Not All Right*.

The more *Not All Right* you have been, the more relief and rightness you feel.

But was it worth putting yourself through all that, for this?

The other three were somewhere else going through their own process.

They were re-hydrated. Kind of. The famous sweet and milky Nepali chai they were looking forward to never happened.

They were out of milk. And sugar. So they loaded the tea with ginger. So much ginger that it burned on the way down.

Seamus was the first to be able to speak. "I've had worse," he said with a grin and bravely offered his cup for a refill. That's the spirit that built the Empire. Except Seamus wasn't going to slaughter them when he'd had all the tea he could drink.

So Ed was sitting on the rock. The only item the village was selling this time was flip-flops. Made in China. Hmmph!

His musing was interrupted by the sight of an excruciatingly beautiful young woman approaching down the road. Long, dark, silken hair gleaming in the sun, jewelled nose-stud on a golden brown face, chin held high, elegant gait, more golden brown skin exposed at the mid-riff, a long skirt and her small, bare feet picking their way along the dusty path. No hallucination. This was real!

What is so appealing about civilisation? Who needs it? Maybe happiness is peeling off this wet gear and living here forever?

He was still sitting there on the rock when The Goddess came back up the road, this time with an infant on each hip, flies in their eyes and snot streaming from their nostrils. She hawked up something from deep in her lungs and expelled it into the dirt.

❖

The lads made it to The Plains and found a restaurant.

For the first time since the night before the trip they were a team. Now at last they could enjoy the adventure. *Now* it had been fun.

Living The Big One lie had made the whole trip more dramatic. But at the end of the day they were just left feeling a bit stupid. It would have been better to have known the truth all along.

Ed considered the mad rush at the start to avoid the bogus village official for the bogus permit. It was all bogus. He marvelled at how The Gurus had perfectly fed their neurosis.

He felt stupid. It would have been better to have known the truth all along.

◆

Ed was sitting with his black tea in Streaky's cabin. Right now his whole life felt like waiting for a Big One that wasn't there.

A better deal? A better future? A vocation, vehicle, vice, an individual or union that would make all the difference?

Maybe the The Big One was just an accumulation of little ones? Moments like this. Comfortable. Calm. No drama.

It was white outside now. Streaky's cabin was in a cloud. Ed would have to wait for the view to reveal itself again.

Ed had an Irish grandmother and a Scottish grandfather. Sometime during his childhood he had heard that when a family emigrated the neighbours kept the turf fire "smoored" and burning for the day they would return. "Once the fire goes out, the house will soon come tumbling down".

It made sense for Streaky to have someone in this house keeping it warm. A lit stove was like the living soul of the house. And he lit the candle on the small table too. It was distressed by the gusts of wind on the outside of the round window. The dancing flame cast shadows. Between the gusts it rested, and the light filled the room.

Streaky had talked about pride and low self-esteem, and gave the image of a pyramid standing on its point. He said how someone could be big and impressive looking, or sounding, without any basis of foundation. More like a feather in the wind.

Ed could see how his own shoulders broadened and his own voice got louder when he had a few beers. Like a genie appearing out of the top of a pint glass...

He made a mental list of genuine heroes of the day, not media sensations who had learned to kick a football or sing a song. The real game-changers were humble, hitting the headlines not

37

because of who they were but *how* they were. The real stars were quietly, over many years, making a genuine difference in the world, with humility, founded on unshakeable belief. Real pyramids. The right way up. Clarifying that made him feel worse.

He shifted in his seat, looked around, and found what he was looking for. A distraction. One hundred and fifty pages of it, mostly photographs. On the shelf at his shoulder was *Everest –. Summit of Achievement.*

BIGGEST ONE

ED flicked through some facts and acknowledgements in the introduction but was held by the smiling portrait of the Fourteenth Dalai Lama of Tibet, who had written the foreword.

While acknowledging Hillary and Tenzing's successful bid to reach the summit in 1953 as *an inspiring and positive example of what human beings can achieve, the result of great planning, teamwork and individual effort*, he also pointed out that it was another instance of human ability to *dominate the world we live in.*

He wrote that while messages of congratulation flooded in from around the world to celebrate this proud achievement, which coincided in Britain with the coronation of Queen Elizabeth II, the Tibetans were struggling to come to terms with the Chinese Communist occupation.

The Dalai Lama wrote that the mountains were sacred to the Tibetans. Rather than climb to the top of them, Tibetans make salutations by offering juniper incense smoke in their direction and piously walking around them.

When climbing a mountain was the only way to complete a journey, Tibetan travellers respectfully added a stone to the cairns at the top of the pass with a shout of "Lha-gyal-lo!" *Victory to the gods!* A mountain was not something to be conquered, but a place where they could meditate undisturbed, and conquer their minds.

Ed looked into the cloud the other side of the glass and listened to the wind. Streaky had talked about Iraq. And oil. And suffering and happiness. And the contradiction. Ed read the Dalai Lama's words again... *the tendency for us to dominate the world rather than conquer our minds*...this was just the foreword but he felt he had finished one book already. Out of respect he got up to make a cup of tea.

❖

The awesome achievement of mapping India and the Himalayas was thanks to generations of cartographic teams facing formidable obstacles – physical, psychological, political and technical. It took years and cost a fortune in lives and money. The project generated the most complex mathematical equations known to the pre-computer age.

In 1856, a mountain inside Tibet called Chomolungma was surveyed from a viewing point in India and was found to be the highest mountain in the world. It was given a new name, Everest, and became an object of obsession.

Tibet had been a blank space on the world map for many years. Its anonymity was now over yet, somehow, only a handful of Westerners made it into Tibet. Until 1904. In 1904 the Brits officially tricked and terrorised their way in so that they could keep a closer eye on other countries looking to expand their borders.

And in 1921 permission was given for the first reconnaissance climbing expedition.

Ed had trekked to Everest base camp, albeit seventy years later, which helped him begin to imagine the uneasy contrast. He could visualise the nomads of Beyeul Khembalung for whom survival was a delicate balance, who had grazed their animals in those high pastures and communed with the natural environment each day of each year for generations.

One morning in 1921, passing their tents, is a line of pale-skinned and hairy mountaineers, self-indulgent hobbyists salivating over their Mountain-prize.

Is it not amazing, Ed thought, how the same object can stimulate quite different responses in human beings?

In 1922 the mountaineers were back, but not for reconnaissance; this was the first expedition to actually climb Mount Everest. One of the conditions on the "passports" granted by the Dalai Lama was "no guns and no killing – including the animals". The animals were not hunted and the mountaineers remarked on how tame the wildlife was. However, seven Tibetan porters were killed during this unsuccessful attempt, swept to their deaths in an avalanche on the slopes leading to the North Col. Dzatrul Rinpoche, the Abbot of nearby Rongbuk Monastery, wrote, "I was filled with compassion for their lot who underwent such suffering on unnecessary work."

Dzatrul Rinpoche was asking the question – Why?

Many observers were asking the question – Why?

And George Mallory provided the famous answer: *Because it is there.*

Two years later in 1924, on the next unsuccessful attempt, George Mallory died *because it is there.*

There was a book mark, a slip of yellow card-paper. Ed turned it to read the handwritten notations:

"All men's miseries derive from not being able to sit quietly in a room alone." – Blaise Pascal.

GM died because he couldn't leave it there.

He died like most of us will, trying to understand that basic human desire - to explore.

We see a mountain, and we need to stand on top of it. The Majesty is lost on us.

40

Like Adam who could not leave the apple on the tree?
We see the fruit as something outside of ourselves and need to
own it. That is where every story begins.

Ed said "Oh" out loud. It was an involuntary sound.

He closed the book on his left hand, holding the yellow bookmark away from himself in his right, and shut his eyes, and hoped his head would not explode.

❖

He paced up and down. Threw sticks on the fire. Sat back in the chair.

He was relaxed. As relaxed as he could be. His right-leg bobbing up and down like a sewing machine.

And his mind was calm, the only calmness he knew, just the standard undercurrent of constant thinking and distraction.

It was a big improvement on the sand-scooping intensity.

❖

Ed went back to the Everest book and Hillary and Tenzing's triumph in 1953. Of course that was not the end of the Everest climbing story — how could it be?

The euphoria was short-lived, the mountaineers were already focused on the next challenge. Next it had to be attempted with route variations and added complications, and without oxygen. Another bookmark:

Each success leaves them thirsty for more.
Like drinking salt-water.
Hardly an accomplishment at all.

And then everyone wanted a go, and the trekking routes began to suffer the effects of mass tourism. Ed had been one of those "white-eyed visitors" looking for a high-point in their life.

The book quoted a Sherpani from Namche Bazar who com-

41

pared westerners to cattle. Happy to wander about aimlessly all day long, constantly getting sick, and how you had to lead them by the nose over difficult terrain or else they fell off the trail. But if you fed them well, they'd produce a lot of milk.

There was a contribution from the leader of an Everest Pollution Control Committee, who also happened to be the Abbot of Thyangboche Monastery, who said, "Practical initiatives and measures for conservation were missing the main point, that only by changing the minds of those who come to Khumbu will they be able to stop the bad effects of tourism."

Ed decided the Abbot of Thyangboche Monastery should be President of the World, not chairman of a litter campaign.

Only by changing the minds. Sometimes when he heard something like that, the shock and awe was enough to open a door, and he could see and feel the validity of that truth. For a moment Ed really understood something. He made a note.

How we think creates so much distress and debris. Arrogance, anxiety and stress manifest in our outer world as ever more clutter and confusion.

He was not the cause, but he was not separate from the cause.

An image came to mind. Rush hour. Stuck in a traffic jam. Shouting and gesticulating at the other cars. Blaming them. Them who are shouting and gesticulating at you. We *all* are the traffic. And our mentality is the pollution.

Ed resented these Everest pioneers, maybe because they were a mirror for his guilt. These "conquerors" with their double-barrelled names and public-school attitude were more like gold-diggers than mountaineers.

Then he found in the back of the book an appendix with all the different expeditions and a biography of the team members. Like Theodore Howard-Somervell (1890-1975).

He got a double first in natural sciences at Cambridge and qualified as a surgeon in time to be plunged into the horrors of World War I. As well as being an experienced alpine climber – he was a core member of the 1922 and 1924 teams – he was a talented landscape painter and musician. After the Everest expeditions he turned his back on a prestigious surgeon's job in London and instead worked as missionary doctor in southern India for nearly forty years before retiring to the Lake District. This didn't really fit with the self-indulgent hobbyist picture Ed had been painting. Wanting to climb a mountain did not make someone a bad person, any more than being Tibetan made someone a saint.

Yet still, Ed could see a pattern in his own life. Banging his head against a wall was foolish. Especially after it has been pointed out to him that that was what he was doing.

❖

In the middle of the night. He was half asleep and half awake; there was a steam locomotive thundering through his head. Sometimes his thoughts went in a nonsense loop. Tighter and faster. He scratched his scalp until it bled, nearly. He got out of bed, filled a bucket with cold water and stuck the top of his head in it.

The coolness was delicious.

He left it there for a while. Until he could make a cut. Veer off into some place quiet. Let that heavy monster run on alone into the distance. Give him some blessed rest. He was half asleep, living with a mind he couldn't control.

GREEN ROAD

THE next morning the wind had abated. It was only gusting gale force. The ground was wet but it had stopped raining. There was that special air and light of the first real day of Autumn.

Ed would go the lighthouse.

He filled a thermal mug with tea and put that into his day-pack.

Standing at the gate, to his right, in the direction of the light-house, the road was green, there were sheep grazing on it. To his left, in the direction of the village, the road was tarred. Ed turned right.

As he began along the Green Road, he saw ruins of home-steads. And fields, some just garden-sized, separated by moss-covered, broken-down walls.

Why hadn't Streaky renovated one of these ruins, or built on one of the flat parcels of land? Was he hiding from prying eyes, or building without permission?

As he came round the ridge, the lighthouse came into view – maybe another mile, or a small bit more. He would have his tea here.

Another mile...

It reminded Ed of the conversation he had in a bar on the drive out West. The barman was giving him directions and was estimating the distance.

"It's forty miles by our estimation but by yours it'll be a little further." A woman called and the barman disappeared out the back leaving Ed scratching his head. Literally.

A man with a white beard sitting on a stool at the end of the bar, who also did not have a local accent but had clearly made himself at home, came to the rescue.

"There's a saying the further you are from Dublin the longer the miles. That could be because Dublin was within The Pale – the name given to area that was directly under English Rule in the Middle Ages – their miles measured the same as the English, which was 5,280 feet. Outside of Dublin, beyond The Pale, everyone still used the Irish Mile of 6,720 feet. Four Irish miles was often equated to five English. Could be where the expression 'a country mile' came from, y'know, meaning a long way. That's just pub talk now, and a bit of my own supposition."

Ed had not noticed that the barman was back behind the pumps. "Y'know, Ben, there could be truth in what you're saying but I heard it was the English that invented the Irish mile so they could take over more land. That sounds truer to me, at least."

Later that evening a man arrived with a guitar and went to "the lonely woman" sitting near the fire. They beamed at each other and there was a warm embrace. She had the voice of an angel. A small part of Ed felt sorry that such talent would not be shared with the world. A growing part of Ed was inspired by the knowledge that surprises are lying hidden everywhere.

Another mile...

In the Everest book it said that when the first mountaineering expeditions asked the Tibetans for direction, none of it made sense when plotted on their modern maps. Until, that is, the mountaineers discovered that the locals measured distances in cups of tea, and that three cups of tea were equivalent to five miles. Making this translation, the expedition's information correlated well with local experience.

Ed took another sip from his thermal mug. Nectar! He studied the space between himself and the lighthouse.

What a world! You can measure distance with the most complex mathematical equations of the pre-computer age, or with cups of tea.

And the question he asked himself was: has all our ingenuity and divide-and-conquer mentality made us more content? *Is it working for us?*

He looked around to check no-one was watching and unlaced his boots. Cool water came up between his toes. He wore his boots like boxing gloves, making fists of his hands so they would stay on, and walked. Jogged a few steps, then a few more. Smaller, quicker steps.

He walked over patches of wet rock or through clumps of reeds or where scree had fallen across the path, and then ran some more. This was not jogging. He was not dressed in fluorescent lycra, with earphones and stopwatch, spongy shoes and pony-tail swinging in the wind.

This was raw, original. Natural! And he was smiling.

At the lighthouse everything was locked up, there was a helipad; no wonder the road was overgrown and collapsing.

Lighthouses are located in places like this for a reason. This Atlantic Ocean looking America-wards is not big. It is vast. Like a cloudless sky is vast. Like not many other things can be. Achingly enormous.

He didn't stay long, he was ready to run back.

He stopped a few times to smile. And pick his way over rough ground.

No two views were the same, but he hurried on. If he rested and relaxed too much, he would have to look into the void.

◆

"Natural means nothing added, nothing taken away. Unaltered. In the beginning take it slow, cut out all the unnecessary stuff, see how simple it can be. Walk a lot. And take a lot of breaks."

That was Streaky's parting advice.

Like a good student – slow, easy, taking breaks – Ed ran up-and-down the Green Road by the cabin. Baby steps – the gentle patter of tiny feet! Every now and then he went too far for too long. Beyond the limit he had set himself. Half of him felt guilty, the other half wanted to go further. He was a boy again, and he had a smile that began in his heart. Spooky how simple it was, no earth-moving change or ball-busting investment.

After three weeks he ran all the way to the lighthouse. His calves burned. So he slowed down, and took smaller steps, and ran back. When he was running he was himself. That was the only way he could describe it. It was primordially right. And addictive.

The next morning, as he swung his feet over the bed and stood up to walk, he sat quickly down again. He was doing too much but he couldn't stop. He wiggled his toes to help the blood flow, and tried again.

3

Whole-istic...Brogues...With Streaky...Bluebottle
Mountain Hut...Flying a Kite...Impatience...Paris

WHOLE-ISTIC

HANGING out at Streaky's place, reading his books and learning to run natural-style was helping Ed unwind, calming his head, giving him some perspective. There was not the same sense of danger about him, he was hurting less.

He had chosen running. It could have been golf or model railways, walking or gardening or washing dishes. Anything that one could approach with interest and openness – with a beginner's mind. And lose one's self.

He had chosen running, or running had chosen him. All he had to do was break into a jog, even think about going for a run, and his inner atmosphere would change.

Streaky had said he believed everyone was fundamentally good, had a fundamental goodness. Ed often felt wretched. He needed to feel better. Running increased his well-being. Running was achievable. For the first time in his life he felt like he had a direction; he may not have been "saved", but at least he was "postponed". Jesus would be pleased.

It was scary too. It was the opposite of being on the terrace in the football stadium – everyone singing the same song. No-one was validating the thoughts and feelings that flooded through him.

Each day, out there on the paths, fuelled by angst and a burning not-knowing, leaving frustration on the trail and putting down blame. He got super-fatigued and crampy. He slept a lot. But when he woke up it was different. A new beginning.

After half-a-mile or half-an-hour there was usually a communion with the road. With himself.

The hills and the headwinds were part of his run. They didn't mess with him, they made him. After he had climbed, fighting for air, trying to make himself small against the wind, he was ready to turn the bend, stand tall, open out. It was all the same run.

Often he went out running feeling like a bag of bolts, leftover, awkward and heavy and rusty dirty and maybe-useful-one-day. Like a bag of bolts, rubbing up against himself and everything else. The running was like emptying this bag of bolts on a clean piece of ground. Some space. See what's there.

In among all the scrap were some jaggedy bits he wished never existed, but they did. Plenty of unremarkable items, and some shiny pieces. Then he would find what he was looking for, maybe find some pairs or make some connections, the exact fit! He would hold onto that; everything else went back in the bag. In this way he could make some sense of it all...

◆

Today it was awkward and klunky. He just had to smile and get round, repeating to himself "nothing is lost". He came to a patch of gravel and tensed up and slowed down and the stones went up into his feet, and he hobbled and puffed until he passed onto the grass.

He ran on a few paces then stopped and turned. He would try that again. This time as he approached the stones he did quick-fire little steps – no sooner was one foot down, it was up, and the next was there for relief, and up...over the gravel feeling light and easy and he is so grateful for the run! So this was another outing that failed to fail him. Not a bad day after all.

50

Some days the image was a knotted fishing line…or a spill of iron filings, grey, flaky, scattered. And even just the thought of running, or of those first few steps, was like placing the filings on a piece of white paper, the momentum was like a magnet beneath the paper that transformed the debris into a butterfly shape. Beauty and purpose was restored. Naturally.

❖

Maybe because his life was quieter – there was less speed and aggression – his dreams were havoc. There was a new one which repeated every night.

As a child, staying at his grandparents house, he had a TV in the bedroom and one night watched the movie *Papillon* while his parents thought he was sleeping. One of the baddies was a huge muscled man with a full-body tattoo, over his face as well. Now he had returned. In the dream grown-up Ed would beat the crap out of this man. No matter how much force and effort went into every punch and kick, the tattooed man's smile was constant. And friendly. Why was Ed beating him up? Ed didn't know, he just knew he had to.

One day he related the dream to himself and resting in the silence that came at the end of his description he came up with his own solution. "I am in no danger, he's not hitting me. I am in no danger. Maybe next time I will just kiss him."

It was out before he had considered it properly, did he even just say that?

That night he had the dream and he was armed with his response. He went to plant a kiss on the swirls of ink that covered the man's forehead, but there was no-one there; this hulking great man had just dissolved through the power of his intention. And he never returned.

❖

There can be a *yes* in your heart. But when the whole world appears to be saying *no* for long enough you even start thinking *no* yourself. But inside of you there is a stubborn little heart pumping *yes*. Sometimes it just needs one other *yes…*

Two clear *yes's* can be enough to drown out a world of *no's*.

◆

One day he got it. He felt like running was opening up some understanding for him, like removing a mask. He was running on the green road, and without trying to be or expecting to be or even wanting to be, he was *in the zone*.

He had just been padding his way up a track on an overcast day and all of a sudden it clicked, it fell into place, mentally *and* physically. When those two line up like friends, that feels pretty damn good.

He might have missed it, or rushed past it, or failed to recognise it except for the flavour, the taste. Which he had known a few times before, which he had invested so much to go back to, which was snowboarding in powder.

This had the taste of snowboarding on Plansegg.

◆

He'd go up the mountain to the resort before the snow arrived in November and only go back down to the valley six months later, in late Spring, with the thaw.

He worked most of those days. Everyone was paid the same but he would show up early and stay late and do the shitty jobs whenever they came up. Just so on those handful of days after the fresh snow had fallen and the sky cleared and the sun shone, he could flake off work and disappear into the heart of it all. And when he eventually came back he'd still have a job. Because he'd start early and stay late and did the shitty jobs.

For example the evening before the Day of Days. He was last out of work and first to leave the bar, buzzing off three beers, going back to his room. Walking *in* falling snow is a certain feeling, walking *on* fallen snow is a special sound. Kicking the flakes off the toes of your boots, the magic ingredients of awareness and anticipation. Not just anticipation for the future, but of now.

Seven hours later he walks back up the same road. The snow is still falling but it is easing off, the sky clearing. Today felt like it could be the Day of Days.

It's dark and quiet. The lifties, wearing their uniform jackets, emerge out of doorways and join the parade. By the time he reaches the lift station there's a small crowd.

Ed takes a bubble on his own. He doesn't want to share cigarettes and grumble about all the snow that needs shovelling. Not today. And he wants the windows open.

January. The best days are always in January when the cold nights are long and the cold days are short. Excitement building, could easily go into overwhelm, he knows these opportunities only come round once a season; who knows, maybe once a lifetime.

He checks his pockets again and his gloves, helmet, goggles and looks over his bindings. It's all there. Window open is good. The freezing air helps to bring sharp awareness, acclimatise, moderate adrenalin, regulate excitement. He looks down at the perfect white. Infinite possibilities await. He exhales, tries to tune into the naturalness. No thing to force, no thing to want, no thing missing. Nope, can't, too excited!

Ed emerges from the bubble wearing everything he's got and crosses to the chair lift. Rides that one to the top. The noise of the lift accentuates the silence all around. Slides off the ramp at the top. Standing on the roof of the world, two-hundred and seventy degree panorama. Stamps his boots into the board's bindings, snaps the bindings closed. Breathing. Feeling body.

Release down the mountain. Exhales as he lowers, inhales as he extends. Accelerating down the fall line but inside it's slowed right down…weight perfectly balanced *front & back, toes & heel, left & right,* weightless and speeding. Then it happens: the perfect turn.

In every perfect ride there is a perfect turn. The perfect turn is what makes a perfect ride. Mind spirit body board terrain in perfect harmony. No separation.

WHOLE-ISTIC!

He has wings. He *can* fly! There is nothing like it.

He had a choice. Go back to work now and confess, or spend the day free-riding on Alpkopf, and ask for their forgiveness, again. The answer was waiting for him at the bottom of the slope in the form of Lex the Nose and Man Who Smokes.

"Heeey! Egg it is you. We is thinking it is you and it is you! Egg, the snow is purr-fect over Löwens. Coming you with us?"

❖

Ed had this thin shield of respectability that got him the job, and helped him keep it. He'd already had more jobs than most people have in a lifetime but he'd never been fired, he only ever moved on when *he* was ready.

Keeping moving like this no-one got to know him for too long and he never had to take a good look at himself. When he was sixteen he had talked his way into being an eighteen year-old instructor at an Outdoor Activity Centre in Devon. After a few weeks his boss told him "You're a pain in the arse but not quite enough to get sacked." It was a line he had learned to surf.

Man Who Smokes was not so lucky. He was the only person in the resort's history to have been sacked from the job of low-ranking Lift Operator. All a low-ranking Lift Operator had to do was occasionally shovel snow, and the rest of the time he had to sit in a tiny hut with giant windows at the top of the mountain. If there was a problem with the lift he had to radio a Technician. Man Who Smokes had messed up a few times. The final time he got it wrong the lift had stopped and he didn't notice. When the Technicians called by on a random inspection they saw the lift was jammed and the hut was full of smoke, and billowing smoke. The snow close to the hut had melted.

The Technicians saw Man Who Smoke's snowboard a few feet away standing upright in the snow, which meant he must still be trapped inside. The bravest man stepped forward and, fully expecting his glove to melt on the door knob, he opened the door. And fell back from the blast.

Man Who Smokes came stumbling out with a big smile on his face.

"Heeey! Chef! It's yooou!"

Man Who Smokes was famous for, amongst other things, being the only person in the world to be sacked from the job of low-ranking Lift Operator. Lex The Nose was the only person to ever fail the interview for the job of low-ranking Lift Operator. And Lex's dad owned the lift company!

These guys were hard-core slackers, but if you strapped them to snowboards half-cut and in perfect snow, the world would stop turning just to watch.

◆

Ed had just had the perfect run, but he was in the mood for an even more perfect run.

"Yeah, I'm coming with us," said Ed passing the pipe back.

It would be downhill from here.

Five hours later, the lads were on a planet of their own, they were heading home using the "Dances with Wolves" lift, which meant only one thing. They were going to return to the village "Under The Irons". In this condition Ed was Ninja or nothing – he was quite concerned.

"Under the Irons" was one category beyond the *Locals Only* grade. In the days before Health and Safety was invented this was the original chair-lift up from the village. Now disused, it was just a ghostly line of iron pylons, tree stumps, and saplings – a snow-covered near-vertical runway cut through the forest, from the top of the mountain to the east of the village. Once in motion, acceleration was instantaneous, and stopping nigh impossible. If the rider was caught off-balance and missed a turn, the only option was to take a diversion into forest – which would be thin, crusty snow and slalom poles that can impale you – so the quicker you burst back into the glare of the main drag the better.

They waded through the snow and into the woods and out into the clearing. The old lift operator's hut at the top of "Under the Irons" was still in good condition, and there was a bench out the front which looked out over the valley.

"Let's stopping here for a picnic to enjoying the view and for sphincter calming." Lex disappeared behind the hut and returned a moment later wiping the snow off a bottle of Zipfer Marzen. Man Who Smokes got his pipe out. Ed feigned the need for a piss and set off for the tree-line.

The lads patted each other on the shoulder, stepped into their bindings and stood in a line on the crest of the slope. If a pin had dropped on the snow they would have heard it. In front of Ed there was only sky, and the top of the first few pylons were visible, like headstones in a cloud graveyard.

Man who Smokes nudged himself over the edge, followed by Lex.

Here goes…

❖

When someone returned to the village "Under the Irons" they didn't say too much. It was in their eyes. Maybe later in the bar you would hear how it went.

One day Mattie D didn't come back. It was late already, the lifts were closed, there were no responsible, sober people left around. The lads went home via the bar. He had gone missing before, he'd probably show up the next morning with his arm in the air twirling a pair of panties around his index finger.

At noon the following day there was still no sign of Mattie D. Somehow the lads had to tell Mountain Rescue they were looking in the wrong place without giving the game away.

"That was all a big distraction," mused Ed, catching himself, "which is the story of my life – out there, looking for perfection…"

❖

Ed was stunned to find that Day-of-Days feeling just running up a soggy track on an overcast day in Ireland. What was all that about? Just putting one foot in front of the other. Easy and inexpensive and non-dramatic. Natural running was different. It was the difference between swimming naked and swimming-in-a-woollen-jumper. You will always get someone who says swimming-in-a-woollen-jumper is the most fun – but do they really know what they are talking about?

His feet were feeling like an extra pair of hands…

"What is going on?" Ed asked himself. This was not hippy-dippy bullshit. It was taking it way back. This was as gnarly as it got. Ahh! That's it – it tickles the adrenal gland!

For years Ed was mostly anxious, never knowing where the next adrenalin hit was coming from; or when, or how big it would be. He had survived on over-doses and drought for so long, he had learned to grasp, and snatch and hoard. He would do anything for an accessible, even supply. Natural running was the soft landing. It's rehab for adrenaline junkies!

Ed was a snowboarder; he was familiar with *Peak Experience* already, of course he was. Now he was joining up some dots. Abraham Maslow, who first coined the phrase, said, "The great lesson from the true mystics is that *the sacred is in the ordinary*, that it is to be found in one's daily life, in one's neighbours, friends, and family, in one's backyard."

Maybe, even, in putting one foot in front of the other?

His biographer, Edward Hoffman, says that Maslow eventually felt sure that the more emotionally healthy we are, the greater the likelihood of a peak-experience and also the more frequent such episodes become in the course of day-to-day living. Hey! Maybe Ed was on the path to emotional health!

Maslow also suggested that as we age physically, the intensity of peak moments gives way to a gentler, more sustained state of serenity that he called plateau-experiences. Unlike peak-experiences, he advised, such plateaus can be cultivated through conscious, diligent effort. Hoh! Maybe Ed was just getting old!

Who cares why? That's how he wanted to wake up every morning. Ready to make some perfect steps – as if every day it was going to be first tracks down the mountain.

◆

The last few times, whenever he came back to the cabin along the green road, he would stand at the gate and look at the tarmac road stretching out in front of him, all the way to the village, and beyond.

BROGUES

ED fished around under the bench seat in Mr B for a white cloth bag he was sure must be in there. It was. He felt the contents and knew he had found what he was looking for. He released the drawstring and helped them out. This was their time. In each of his hands he held a sandal, and his mouth made a smile.

"I ready," he said to himself, just like Emily J would say it.

Emily J who would say *Bless me* at the end of every sentence like it was a full stop. Unless the sentence was future tense, in which case the full-stop would be *Godwillin*.

The church was a white-washed bungalow standing on a rocky rise sheltered from the Ocean by a belt of palms and Caribbean pines. The doors were open and fans turned overhead and condensation dripped down the windows. There was a missionary priest there that evening. Ed had arrived in the middle of a song, the place was rocking.

The song ended and a woman in the congregation stood up.

"The sixteenth of December 1986 that was the day I started running for my life…Lord Jesus! I know I don't have a voice but I want us all to hear this." With that the celebrant launches into a song and immediately she has the whole place behind her.

The place was rocking again. Everyone wearing their best clothes. Including jackets and hats.

The song ends to make way for another testimony which is met with a universal *Praise the Lord!*

The lady at the lectern reads out the first line of the next song. The brooch pinned to her black beret says *Jesus* in glittery letters. A man clears his throat and spits out the fire exit door. Two guitarists and a drummer start up, after a few bars they are playing the same song, just in time for the voices to blend in. It's loud and it's inspired. And the place was rocking.

Ed had scored a job as caretaker of a field station in the Bahamas during hurricane season. All the American staff were on vacation, but the locals were friendly. Emily was the breakfast cook at the field station. She was seventy-five island-years old, so sweet and kind and quiet and humble and against-the-odds-happy, living in a wooden shed in that belt of palms and pines.

Emily levers herself up from the pew and with her eyes clenched tightly shut, and without waiting for the microphone she sings out "I tell you. I tell *you*! When the Lord comes for Emily Johnson she ready!"

It takes the roof off the place, everyone is shouting at Emily

"Amen!"

"Yes, Jesus!"

"Save me, Jesus!"

Ed resonated with Neil *better to burn out than fade away* Young and James *live fast, die young, leave a good looking corpse* Dean.

Emily *I ready* Johnson was messing with his head. Here was

59

an apparently happy person who was happy to die. Is that not a contradiction?

What did he do next? He met Filo and they went to Benny's Bar. Ed bought them a cold beer each. Then it was Filo's turn; "Let's have cuba libre. You like it strong?…Okay, okay, we just make it half-and-half then."

This was hurricane season. So long as there were no hurricanes, there was nothing to do. The next morning, as the tide turned, they walked to the road bridge over Connor Creek, jumped into the river and floated through the mangrove, down to the ocean. Which is where the crashed plane was.

The story was that the plane was loaded up with drugs, it ran out of fuel and crashed in the shallows, just offshore from Benny's wooden shack. The bloodied pilot disappeared into the jungle with what little he could carry. Benny had the rest. When the gangsters arrived Benny pointed in the direction of the pilot's escape. They beat Benny up and threatened his family and smacked him about some more before leaving, their honour intact, and now Benny lived in a brick house and had a bar near the beach.

Filo helped Ed make his own pair of sandals from some left-over aeroplane tyre – "Cos he got no metal in him," Filo said as they went about cutting out the footprint.

There was no hurricane that year, a few were forecast, one came close but tracked away at the last minute. That was years ago. The tyre-sole was a good as ever. Ed had replaced the paracord straps a few times, now he was using climbing tape with plastic buckles to keep the tension.

He had never thought to run in these. Works with or without shoes, Streaky had said.

"I ready," Ed said to himself, pulling on his sandals. "I ready to take this show on the road."

WITH STREAKY

ED was on his way back from the village Post Office. A shape morphs out of the mist. Even from a distance there is an ease in that posture and in that movement.

He runs without a watch. And today no shoes. He is not trying to lose weight or build muscle, and doesn't seem to have any worries. He breathes easily.

"By all means run with your thoughts,
but watch how you do.
If you don't hold onto them,
they'll slip away, get left behind,
and it'll just be me and you.
Dark is the day
when thoughts and emotions steal your mind,
robbing you blind."

He's like all the eccentric people Ed had ever met; the difference is, he's not trying. No attitude, no affectation, no pretence.

It's not acting out, it's freedom from inhibition and it comes naturally. He makes alternative feel mainstream. Everything can be as it is. Including Ed.

Streaky was half crazy, perhaps, but the other half more than balanced him out.

Over his breathing he says :

"Lighten up!
We live like the man
as poor as a mouse
the whole day sad
in his ruin of a house.
The man died never knowing
of the riches overflowing
in his basement."

Silence for a few seconds, then,

"Midas touch is not turning base metals into gold,
it's in seeing the treasure we hold
in the palm of our hand
when grasping fingers unfold."

Many of Streaky's lines and verses went over Ed's head, or were missed because he was still pondering whatever came before, but it didn't seem to matter. He was learning to leave it there, he could make sense of it later – or not.

"What a weather! Last night's rain smells good, no? Let's take the bog road."

Ed told him about his recently recurring dream, the one with the train. All he knows is, he has to get on, he doesn't know where it's going to, and once he's on he can't get off.

"Until the dream ends, right? Until you wake up? When you wake up you recognise the dream as a dream. You are free of it."

"Well yeah, s'pose."

A little later Streaky starts up. "People run, how they live, heavy and oblivious. That's why they get hurt. Run natural-style, find your form, a style that works for you. It teaches balance, balanced people are better runners, and have a happier time generally. It's worth the effort. It'll work for you anytime and everytime, anywhere and everywhere, with or without shoes."

❖

Ed had pieced together some of Streaky's back story from snatches of conversation;

"My folks were Scottish. They sold their corner shop in England. They told their toddler son they were sailing away to find some nice people.

"Somewhere along the south coast of Ireland Dad struck up a conversation with Bernie, a ham radio enthusiast from the village, who told us that it was regatta day in the town that Saturday. We sailed into the harbour at mid-morning on the Saturday and Bernie met us off the boat. I had spent most of the voyage strapped to the lifeline puking my guts up while my parents sailed the boat. I was so grateful to Bernie. He was the reason I wasn't at sea anymore.

"Do you have chips in Ireland? I asked him, because the fish we had been catching didn't come with chips. We had been eating from tins and packets. I had been dreaming of chips."

"The next day Bernie invited us to his place for a barbecue. In his back garden he had rigged up a deep-fat fryer. I can still taste those chips, they are still the best chips I have ever eaten. Dad had found his nice people."

They lived on the boat through the winter, sold it in the Spring and bought some land.

"Growing up, I had no understanding of what it was to rebel, there were no borders, nothing to rebel against. It was a sign of the times as well as my upbringing. I was taught to recognise right from wrong and encouraged to stay within that.

"If you can't help, at least don't harm. What you do and say and even think is your responsibility.

"In those days, living here, your neighbours were your support network, your fortune was not separate from theirs. It was so clear. Their well-being was in your own interest.

"Life was hard. Without your neighbour it would be impossible.

"I can't remember if we had electricity when I was young. We must have at least had lights because it was very exciting when there was a power cut. Then the candles would come out. We washed our clothes in the river. I remember that. And going to school aged eight in a tweed waistcoat and matching kilt that my mother had made. I didn't like it but not enough to protest; it was never an issue for me, so it never became an issue.

"I was the only non-Catholic in school, that didn't seem to bother me either. Once they had a Mass in the school and I did the reading, and after that the class filed up to the priest standing at the front, so I joined the line but when I got to the front the priest didn't give me the wafer. But that was not dramatic or traumatic at all, this is probably the first time I have even recalled it.

"My awareness was in the world not in myself. I did not think so much, I did stuff.

"I have no memory of being bored. It never occurred to me. These days things are more controlled. We control the temperature in our houses, and in our fridges, and the humidity and the airflow and the movements of our children. And the results are quite uncontrollable. How we lived then, *inside* and *outside*, was less clear, it was all the same place, so I just went outside and stuff happened. Other families lived a few miles away so it was mostly just me and my sister. Or just me. Going barefoot through nature was adventure enough. There were dens and special places and everywhere in between.

"The roads were not tarred but the surface was good. Cars were rare, so I would run after them, waving and shouting, and see how long I could keep them in sight. That was when I was younger. Later it was different.

"The driver would look in the rear-view mirror and I'd be close enough to see the passengers turn and the car swerve a small bit. Eventually I would collapse to the side of the road. Or so they thought! I'd dive through the hedge for any sort of short-cut -- the best was at the top of The Gap – I'd race up through the forestry, down Driscoll's fields, across the stream and scramble up the rise, west along the mine's track, and when the car rounded the bend, they'd see me vaulting the gate, gazelling down the middle of the road, and they would have to slow down and marvel at the boy who could run faster than they could drive. Coming into the village, I would hold the pace but pull over into the side a small bit. They would not pass me out

64

straight away, there was always a pause…

"'What will this eejit do next?' they'd be asking themselves.

"Eventually they would accelerate past. As many people as there were in the car, there would be that many dropped-jaws. Maybe a camera too.

"For a couple of summers I was a tourist attraction. In those days Donny worked behind the bar in The Lighthouse, and he would tell me how the visitors would be shouting about 'The Throwback Kid' who could run from town to the village faster than they could drive it. *'I kid you not, Ethel got a picture. Barefoot! In a skirt!'*

"At the end of one summer my sister and I were sent to the city on the Harringtons' bus to buy our school uniforms for the new term. We came back with two kayaks. For the following year we went to school in trousers that were too short, and shirts that pinched our necks, but when we came home the kayaks were waiting. We had already taught ourselves to abseil and climb, now our playground included the sea.

"The land had always been sacred to me, but it is only through leaving, and then coming home, that I became conscious of the gravity of that connection. After living by the sea, it's very difficult to not live by the sea. Especially a sea with tides, and a wind that brings the four weathers each and every day. And these fields filled with stones, and the stone walls that separate them, have a heartbeat, don't you think?"

❖

Ed didn't want to be anywhere else. He was liking living in the cabin. Loving it mostly. Not knowing how long it would last for, if this would be his last week, or day even, gave the whole experience a delicious edge. Ed appreciated the time.

Ed never found Streaky. Streaky found him, usually at the beach, usually in the morning, just appearing out of nowhere, before disappearing to who-knows-where.

He didn't want to ask Streaky what the deal was or how long he could stay; it never seemed to be the right time, and he might not like the answer, and there was always other stuff to talk about.

BLUEBOTTLE

ED told Streaky about the afternoon he arrived at the beach in Mr Blanco. He'd been driving since before dawn. He was dog-tired. He set up the bed and closed a few curtains to keep the sun out. He laid himself down, body heavy, eyelids dropping, head hitting the pillow, eyes closing and…and a big bluebottle fly came buzzin' in. Buzzin' loud like a mad thing. Buzzin' from one corner to the next, from floor to roof, barely a pause as it hit off the walls and bounced on the window. Non-stop. Then it landed on his nose. He flicked at it and it was off again. Filling the room. On and on. More and more. Manic.

Then it found the same open window and it buzzed off. Finally peace.

Dogs barking in the very distance and children calling some-where, the curtains moved gently, a spider walked…P-E-A-C-E.

"Bluebottle buzzing," mused Streaky. "That's how mind is, like the fly, buzzing all the time. Full of static noise. Except we are so used to it we don't notice, we don't feel ourselves tiring, there is always so much to think about and do. *Too much* to think about and do, and all the time knowing we need to relax, to take a break.

"The only break we are ever going to get is the one we take right now. Take a break where? In our mind. There is even a way to be spacious and relaxed while in the midst of activity, without dropping anything. Would that not be a skill worth acquiring? Especially in this modern world, which is so fast and complex and full. Finding stillness in movement may be our only option."

Ed was lapping this up. Outwardly he was a uniquely lucky person – he had lived a fortunate life, he could appreciate that. It was becoming clear that most of the difficulties he had experienced came from an over-active, under-understood mind. He had agonised over scenarios that never materialised, about words that were never said, about things that were without substance, about a future that never arrived. So his mind was often full of difficulties that did not exist, except in his mind. And that mind was the filter of his everyday experience. No wonder his life was often confused.

He was already suspecting that happiness was not getting something else, but being content with what you have. He was now considering that wisdom was not the *addition* of knowledge but the *release* of anxious reflection and endless speculation.

Streaky gave the example of the waves of Tibetan refugees arriving in India, Sikkim and Bhutan, and the West, some of whom were removed from extremely comfortable and privileged lives, where they were respected, venerated even; how they could lose their family and friends and wealth, perhaps spend twenty years in a concentration camp and yet remain mentally clear and strong. Even live happily, with compassion for their oppressors.

"They are our example. While mind can be the source of difficulties, with the right training it can also help us overcome them. If we want to escape a cycle of hyper-activity, or frustration, or anything, we need to draw a line or make a cut, to find an end, a thread, a place to begin. We need to make a cut."

This was resonating with Ed. He told Streaky about his night in the hut on the mountain in Austria. The night that proved that being on his own was one person too many.

MOUNTAIN HUT

THERE was a time when Ed was spending the whole year in Austria: winters in the ski resort, summers rafting in the valley. But then the tapestry had begun to unravel, and he knew he was facing his last summer of river-guiding. One of the new generation of guides arriving from Nepal via London brought a copy of *The Tibetan Book of Living and Dying* with him, which Ed borrowed while the new guide finished an Ian Banks novel.

It was a fat book, but Ed read it fast. He was three chapters into a second read before he had to give it back. He had lots of free time because even before the tourists arrived he had suffered a nasty cut on his forearm in an after-hours, alcohol-fuelled incident.

The lads had carried the half anaemic and fully pissed casualty to the door of the village doctor who was a Nazi. Really. He had the uniforms and the hair-cut and everything. On top of that, an English raft-guide had gotten his eldest daughter pregnant several years before.

They rang the doctor's door bell in the early hours of a Sunday morning and legged it, leaving Ed bleeding on his doorstep.

Seglinde was the waitress at the pizzeria which also had a little corner bar. She kept the left-over pizzas on the side for the lads to collect when they came in for their Jägermeister nightcap. When she heard Ed had been delivered to Doctor Ulrich she kicked them all out of the bar, straightened her dirndl in the glass door, nodded at the portrait of the hero rebel Andreas Hofer on the wall and stormed off down the street. She found Ed in a downstairs "surgery" that no-one knew existed; he was about to have his arm amputated. He had his E111 insurance form jammed in his mouth and had re-dislocated his left shoulder trying to free himself.

The whole incident left Ed a little traumatised and he couldn't work, so he spent a lot of time on the river bank watching the world float by. One day walking back up to the raft base he had the feeling he was not walking anywhere. He was staying in the same spot, lifting his feet up, and the planet was turning under him.

When he got back up to the village he heard himself telling the other guides. They stared back at him.

"Hark at him!" said Davey Train. "Scrambles, you don't half spout some shit."

Very secretly they were ashamed that they were nearly accessories to murder and that Seglinde was the only person man enough to rescue Ed.

The doctor had been shipped off to a secure hospital in Switzerland. Ed was living in a cabin in an apple orchard owned by Gretel, Seglinde's mother. Gretel's family included a small husband, two huge sons and Seglinde. Ed was invited to join them every Sunday for pie and cream.

Ed went to the bars less. Most nights he would be asleep before closing time, only to be woken by the other guides throwing apples at his hut. Until they broke a window and Gretel set her sons on them.

A month after the drama he did go out and was at the bar with a ski instructor who had opted to spend the summer drinking last winter's wages. The ski instructor was telling Ed about a hut on the south side of the mountain where a priest spent the summer. He wouldn't be there yet, too early in the year, and except for him it would only ever otherwise be a refuge for hunters caught out by a winter storm, so it was certainly unoccupied now. It was an amazing spot, like the rooftop of the world.

It was early evening, Ed had the day off tomorrow, so he took a receipt out of his back pocket and asked for a pen to take down some directions.

Logging road. Yep. Klamsteig as far as the cross. Yep. Red

route. Right before the landslip. Big tree struck by lightning, fork right. Yep.

"Then you are about half way," said the ski instructor.

"Hang on, I'll ask for more paper."

"Don't bother. I don't know any more. I haven't been there. But it can't be that difficult to find: a small meadow on the south side, 200 metres below the summit. The mountain gets smaller the higher you go."

"No shit! Learned that in your mountain guides exam did you?"

The ski instructor looked at Ed while she drained her glass and pushed it towards him. One good turn begets another. Always. Has to. Why else would you help anyone?

The other guides arrived from the Hackl's Keller and heard what was going on.

Well, for a start, the hut didn't exist, and even if it did it was in a different place, on a different mountain, you'll never find it, a few of us have tried, the forecast is shit *and* there's a party above the Rathaus. So let's go! Ed may have let the idea slide if it wasn't for the *you'll never find it*.

He feigned enthusiasm for the party and slipped out the back door. On his way home he met Tommi, Gretel's eldest boy who had just finished work – he was employed on building sites substituting for cranes and bull-dozers. Ed told Tommi about the party and suggested he remind the Englander raft guides that if the hut was damaged again it wouldn't just be Tommi and his brother coming round to slap some sense into them; Gretel had promised to come looking for them herself...

Ed slept soundly till just before dawn. On the step he found some "shwechkin cake" wrapped in foil. He put it in the top of his pack and left the village by the logging road.

After nearly four hours of walking uphill he took shelter under a broken, blackened tree. It had either been bombed or

70

struck by lightning. It was raining but not heavy and the wind was light and it didn't look like it was going to get any worse – a good day on the mountain.

He ate the cake. It tasted good. He rolled a cigarette and smoked it with relish. Wet-day cigarettes were always the best. The busted-up tree was his last reference point. He was at a cross-roads.

Down was a hot meal, warm bed and cold beer. And ridicule. Up was…up was something else. A bird called, it sounded like a laugh. Yes, hahah!

The sweat cooled on his back. He would keep going. He took the right fork, up, with tree roots for steps he climbed the steep forest track.

The rain had been heavy for an hour; his shorts sagged impressively around his knees, and the wind was gusting gale force. Paths appeared and disappeared. Began with hope and ended at a cliff edge. At one point the mist cleared and he could see the village below.

He quoted Nietzche quietly to himself: "He who seeks may easily get himself lost, it's a crime to go apart and be alone – thus speaks the herd."

He circled and back-tracked and climbed again. For the last time now, he would beat a hasty retreat if this path was a dead-end.

Then he saw a cross. A crucifix. The Lord Jesus crucified in the heart of the forest. There was a bench, which on a bright clear day could be a pleasant place to sit, and a path to the left, traversing round and up the mountain. He saw an ibex, it saw him and walked slowly away. There was an acre of meadow and a moment of celebration as he saw the hut, and saw there was no smoke coming from the chimney. He broke into a jog. The door opened easily and he ducked inside. Dry wood, hay, matches. Sweet Jesus!

The light outside had faded by the time the water started to boil. He sat there in his underpants with his sleeping bag over his shoulders. His clothes were spread over the wood stacked against one wall. He wedged the door shut and added his pants to the pile. He hoped they'd dry quickly. If a hunter arrived looking for shelter, he'd feel a bit more comfortable opening the door with pants on.

The hut was made of tree trunks. It was just one small room, one door, no windows. Opposite the door was an open hearth, two beaten pans, an iron skillet, a knife and a spoon, and the stool he was sitting on. The bed was a waist-high shelf to his left. The rest of the space was crammed with dry, ready-to-fry fire-wood.

He made tea, ate chocolate and lit a cigarette. The thunder and lightning was on top of him as he inhaled the smoke, and exhaled smoke, mindfully. Maybe that was as much the attraction of smoking as the nicotine. At least part of it.

Rescued by the end of another day. But relaxing for more than a few moments was a challenge. Without the stress that held him together he felt uneasy and got busy again. Gusts of wind whistled through the gaps between the roughly hewn timbers. He plugged some of the bigger gaps but only succeeded in changing the tune.

He rolled into the straw of the shelf bed and slept quickly, dreaming that the wood pile avalanches onto the hot embers and blocks the door. He is trapped, he feverishly re-stacks the wood but it's too late, it blazes into flame, the hut becomes a funeral pyre…he is attending his own cremation.

He watched through the gaps in the beams as the night lightened. The storm was over. He hadn't slept since he woke from the nightmare. The activity involved in making a breakfast of tea, chocolate and a cigarette was a relief after hours of lying physically inert with a revving mind. No need to look for the spring; a pot lying under an eave was to-the-brim with the night's rain.

Outside the air was fresh, the long grass was soaked, two deer looking, an eagle wheeling, and behind the hut was the wet, freshly cut cliff where the night's thunder and lightning had halved the mountain, or so it looked.

He looked in the opposite direction, at the mountains across several valleys, and at the pasture in front of him and . . . Jaysus . . . is that the Preacher appearing over the rise, a long black coat, and a black wide-brimmed hat? *Who's been sleeping in MY bed!?* Help! He'll baptize me to within an inch of my life.

He blinked, there was no-one there, but the feeling that someone or something was just around the corner would not go away...

He exhaled, had one last go at enjoying the peace and beauty. Even in perfect stillness this mind is still a box of frogs. Especially then.

Ed would not have been able to express what he felt right then. This was hard. A defeat. Deep down he had discovered that he could be in the perfect place, in the middle of creation, the most excellent blend of ying and yang, but still be looking at it from the outside. That's pain.

He threw the last swallow of his second cup of tea into the grass. Didn't even finish that. Filled up a water bottle and picked up his bag, made sure the fire was out and the door was firmly closed behind him and set off for the valley. And familiarisation.

Five minutes later he nearly turned back. Was he sure the fire was out? And the door firmly shut? Moving in this direction, increasing the distance between him and it, he could look back and enjoy it. It did not threaten him any more. He decided he was in awe, even fearful of anyone who would *chose* to spend three months a year living there alone.

He remembered a line he had written out from Nietzche, hoping it would one day mean something: "One man runs to his neighbour because he is looking for himself, and another because he wants to lose himself. Your bad love of yourselves makes solitude a prison to you."

Mean something? He had just lived it!

He knew lots of people who fancied themselves but that was different. What could be more important than loving yourself? What could be harder?

There must be a knack to it.

FLYING A KITE

"THAT'S a perfect line from Nietzche." Streaky was enjoying himself. "There's a real irony here. We tend to be very self-centred and cherish our own interests, yet often we don't like ourselves. Or maybe we are very self-centred and cherish ourselves *because* we don't like ourselves.

"Whatever, the fact is we do hurtful things when we are hurting inside. The Buddha says something like, *You can search throughout the entire universe but you will never find anyone who is more deserving of your own love and affection than you are yourself.* It's the crucial first step.

"You deserve your love. It is unreasonable to expect others to care for and respect you if you don't care for yourself. Sure, we all have weaknesses and make mistakes but those are things we can change. We need to look at, accept, befriend and love ourselves."

The piece that really made an impression on Ed was when Streaky said that in order to go for a picnic with yourself, you have to like yourself, even just a little bit. You have to be able to relax with who and how you are right now. Streaky said how he had found himself in a place where he didn't like who he was, what he had become; the happy child had been corrupted. In

74

order to spend some quality time on his own there needed to be some acceptance, a space in his attitude. He had to turn down the volume and ignore the commentary that said it was a waste of time and so was he. He took a pledge to suspend judgement, to create an atmosphere of gentleness, of understanding.

"Take that step. It's easier said than done. Lots of doubts came up for me like – does this not contradict the fundamental message of all authentic spiritual traditions? Surely a meaningful life is one of generosity and kindness, of service, *to others?* What can loving yourself accomplish? Then I found the Buddha also said, *He who truly loves himself can never harm another.* That's when I came to see how it was like an inner disarmament. It's the path to ultimate peace. Within and without.

"It is because there is confusion and hurt on the inside that we cause harm to ourselves and others. So when we truly love ourselves we do not harm others. And, importantly, others cannot harm us. We move beyond harm.

"Christians say 'charity begins at home', *maybe* this is another interpretation of that.

"This is the first step, creating a spacious attitude toward ourselves, and our world. This LOVE thing is so important when we start to spend time with ourselves. Being gentle and kind and patient and skilful is essential if we are to make any progress.

"You know, at 6am each day the miners of this village would begin a twelve-hour shift descending, perhaps for hours, along a systems of ladders and tunnels, ever deeper. They would often navigate their way in complete darkness – they had to pay for all their tools and equipment – so only on arriving at the rock-face would they light a precious candle, sticking it to their helmet with a lump of clay. Imagine that feeling. Finally, illumination.

"What made me think of it now is, in a draft a candle flame jumps and flickers. The flame has to be still for a candle to burn brightly. It's like that with the mind. For clarity we need stillness.

"So after developing some kindness toward ourselves, a second step would be to cultivate stillness. The books told me to watch my breath, that *paying light attention to my breathing is one of the simplest but also one of the most profound methods.*

"It seemed to work for everyone else but I found it claustrophobic, I was trying too hard, and my mind just got wilder. I did not know how to pay attention without tension. This is about the time I found myself watching the children fly their kites, and there was my answer. This helped me bring it all together. A kindness, even playfulness, with the stillness. And attention without tension.

"You see, the wind is a constant here, there's almost always a breeze. You can moan about it, or you can surf it. In my head, when I sat still, the thoughts were endless and my emotions had a life of their own. The kids flying their kites inspired an idea. I needed to learn to ride my mind.

"I was sitting here and a boy was flying a kite. The kite was his focus. And the string was his connection to the kite.

"It occurred to me that, if the present moment is my focus, it is my breathing that helps me stay connected. My connection to the present moment is through my breathing. Instead of being the main focus, the breathing could be my connection, it was my 'live link'.

"The string prevents the kite from being lost. The breath prevented my awareness from being carried away. This is simple, but don't be fooled by the simplicity. Some things we reject because they are too simple. Other things we reject because they are too difficult. We are left with nothing. This works! By simply being mindful of the present moment or my current action, with the support of my breath, I had entered another world.

"I found I could give the kite, which represents the focus, about a quarter of my attention.

A second quarter of my attention was on the string, or my breathing, acting as my watchful awareness, keeping me present, making sure I was not carried away. Which left the other half resting, spaciously abiding with whatever else was happening - the people on the beach and the sky and the diving birds. And I was smiling.

"The kite is just an example, but a neat one. I tried it while walking, and talking, and washing the dishes. Whenever my breath accompanied the action, it freed my mind. It was a very open and awake place to rest.

"If my mind is calm I can *let out more string*, and let more of the world in without being distracted. I am mindful of the present action but not at the expense of everything that is happening around me – and the sky above me. When cloud-like thoughts and emotions drift into view, if I pay them no special attention they float on by. If I stay lightly and mindfully aware of the present moment, the kite and my connection to it, the string, which is my breathing, then the thoughts and emotions can float on by.

"Of course I am often distracted, but when I realise I have been distracted that's the *training moment*. Without any judgement or commentary I begin again, connect to the present moment through the breathing. With kindness and vigilance.

"If I let my kite out too soon and too far, I say meditation does not work. Like natural running can cause injury if you do too much too soon, if you run before you can walk."

Streaky was inspiring. He made a small splash like only a good swimmer can. To be that casual takes a lot of confidence.

❖

Ed needed to be patient. Begin slowly. He found that calming and focussing his mind while remaining aware of his breathing for even fifteen minutes each morning would be enough to change the whole day.

He likened this morning meditation training to making a flask of tea. At different times of the day, whenever he wanted or needed to, he could dip back into it, he could take a sip.

IMPATIENCE

ED had gotten into the habit of going to bed soon after dark and waking up an hour before first light. What a luxury!

It was dark now but he couldn't sleep. Definitely not sleepy now. He got out of bed and made tea and spread nutella on oatcakes. He lit a candle and sat in the chair with his sleeping bag pulled around him and sipped and munched. Like a king. Aaaahh! He waited for relaxation to find him. Aaah!

Ah screw it! He was irritated and agitated. Everything was in place – nutella and tea and his sleeping bag and the candle light and nothing to do in the morning – but it wasn't happening.

10.17pm. He thought about calming his mind with some Kite Meditation. He just thought about it. No. He knew what was disturbing him. It was the free newspaper he'd picked up in the city maybe two months before, the paper that was behind the seat in Mr B. Wasn't there, on the front page of that, wasn't there some mention of a "Waterfront Marathon"?

When he had picked up the paper he wasn't a runner, he wasn't interested.

Now he was. And he was.

He threw off the sleeping bag, slapped his feet into his brogues and crossed into the shed and up the steps. He looked at the front page under the pale glow of Mr B's door-open light. The column strip along the top of the front page read:

West Cork Wayfarer returns from trans-globe voyage Page 3.

Your garden this Autumn Page 11

This year's Waterfront Marathon Page 23.

He shivered, more with anticipation than cold, stuck the paper under his arm, slid the van door closed, shimmied down the steps back into the cabin, dove under the sleeping bag, folded two oatcakes into his mouth, took a swig of tea, and turned to page 23. It was the inside back cover and a small-bit greasy.

Most scenic marathon…international field…accomplished athletes and first time… fill out the form…closing date midnight Friday 16th November. Friday 16 November?

He looked at his watch. 16/11. Today. Tonight.

This was Ireland. Ed decided that if he had his entry in the post box by midnight he would qualify.

Just one problem. He was due to fly back to Wales for Harris's birthday exactly around that time. He checked the dates: the marathon was on Saturday 6th December, the return flight to Ireland was…he fished out the shoebox from under the futon, found his passport and opened the folded paper that was tucked into it…his return flight to Ireland was Friday 5th.

This is going to happen!

Another mouthful of tea and oatcakes. Aaaahh!

He would have to go from prancing up and down the road to marathon runner in three weeks. He was psyched! He did not pause to ask, "What's all this about?"

Nothing about it ticked the boxes for why he was running. It was a contradiction. It would probably just be one of those mistakes that becomes a story that got longer and better with each recitation. Ed's life sounded good in hindsight. Maybe it was time he had a marathon story.

Actually, Ed already had a marathon story but it had been archived under another heading, in another file, probably because it didn't have so much to do with running.

PARIS

TEN years earlier Ed drove to Paris from South Wales in his first VW Camper Van, with fellow students Ando, Stu and Lithe Girl. The attraction was Lithe Girl, and an adventure, it was not the running.

Passing the Student Union Bar they were waved down by a friend-of-a-friend who leaned in the window, saw Lithe Girl, and asked their purpose. This person guaranteed he knew where his passport was and, if they passed his house, he'd be in-and-out-in-a-minute and would share petrol costs. He probably just wanted a lift home and the chance to sit next to Lithe Girl. They let him in and drove to his house and waited ninety seconds before mirror, signal and manoeuvre into the afternoon traffic and into second gear and ... the slide-door opened and yer man commando rolled into the back with a little red book in one hand and a tooth brush and a bag of crisps in the other.

These were the days when nothing mattered. They had no idea what they were getting into. No-one had done any proper training or preparation – which was usual – their bodies were young and their minds immune.

They were unable to sit still, or socialise or do anything really, unless they were drinking and smoking. They arrived in Paris a bit pissed and slightly stoned and decided to go drinking and smoking. They were having so much fun they no longer cared who slept next to Lithe Girl. Oh shit! Where was Lithe Girl? The Student's Union are not going to like this one bit, and she's probably got parents. They were relieved to find Lithe Girl safely locked inside the van that was parked illegally near race headquarters.

Phew! They slept on park benches roughly surrounding the van.

Not even 8 o'clock and very hot. Lithe Girl looked sensational! The weather was beautiful too. Time to get their game-face on. They needed to find some water, breakfast and the start line. They found water.

Regarding breakfast, they were not runners *per se* but any eejit knew diet was crucial. Paris was not good at supermarkets. Lithe Girl managed to find half a litre of pulverised fruit while the lads found a bakery where yesterday's twenty-two inch strawberry flans were on special offer. They had one each.

They found the start line.

Now it was really hot. There were a lot of people, running through baking streets and, occasionally, leafy avenues…Ed got separated from the others…at the half-way point he was on course for a sub-three hour marathon…

His next memory was Parisian Strawberry Flan.

Another one was stopping in a tunnel under the River Seine, it was blissfully cool. He pissed a small black worm of urine that held its shape as it hit gutter, and wriggled off.

Lithe Girl picked them up one at a time from the finish line and drove them home.

After that Ed hung up his trainers. Metaphorically speaking. Actually they were covered in blood – they never did fit him very well – so he binned them.

❖

Ed sat in candlelight, ten years older but no wiser, filling out a marathon entry form. He sealed and stamped the envelope. To-night was the closing day, he wanted to post it before midnight; it wouldn't get there any sooner but he was not ready for sleep, and was feeling like a bit of a run – after all he had some training to do…

❖

They were all talking at once, walking in a huddle, sharing a coat that they held over their heads, splashing through puddles. On the other side of the road a figure in sandals ran under one of the few street lamps in the village.

The group stopped walking and talking. "Crazy fecker!" one of them called out. Okay. Ed was out running, alone, late on a Friday night, in the wind and the rain. In November in home-made sandals. A beginner runner on his way to the post box with his marathon entry in a plastic bag in his chest pocket. Running to the post box so he could send it before midnight. Okay. They had a point. Mad.

Ed had a shower when he got home. And slept well. And woke up early. Smiling. Maybe not so mad after all.

◆

As he slipped the envelope into the post box he felt remote. This was a long way west of the rest of the world.

His half-baked marathon entry mission reminded him of the story of how the miners were paid. At peak production there were more than 1,500 of them and they were supported over-ground by the men, women and children who were crushing and concentrating the ore, and there were teams of carpenters, and herds of horses were used for transportation, so blacksmiths to keep them on the road. It was a massive operation. Everyone was paid a pittance but if you added it all together it became a small fortune. On the pay-days transporting money from the bank in the city out this far was a risky business. Too dangerous to send a courier, and sending money by post was no safer. The solution was to cut the big bank notes in half, and send one half of all the notes with the messenger and the other half of all the notes by post. Then at the local bank they would be rejoined and exchanged for small notes and coins to pay the workmen.

Ed liked that.

4

Harris…When Harris Met Ed…Cat's Story
Land of My Fathers…Marathon

HARRIS

ONE week before the marathon, Harris and Cat picked Ed up from the airport.

"Where to 'ave ewe been this time?" asked Harris.

Ed said he'd been detoxing on the west coast of Ireland and he was just visiting for a week because he had this marathon coming up.

"Tidy darts!" said Harris. "We're going to the pub anyway. It's my birthday, that's why ewe've come, and everybody knows that generations of Welsh rugby teams 'ave performed magnificently following week-long drinking sessions. Cat's been looking forward to it too," he added with finality. So that was decided.

They had been sitting in Harris's van looking at the flashing red lights at a level crossing for several minutes with no sign of a train. "It would be quicker to walk," said Ed

"I doubt it," said Harris. "If we were at the crossing in St Fagan's it *could* be quicker to walk. But we're not. We're lost in a foreign country, keep ewer doors locked, ewe've seen the movies."

Harris was agitated. Aer Lingus had cut the Cork-Cardiff route so Ed had to fly to Bristol, which is in England. Harris had agreed to pick him up because Bristol was spitting distance from the Welsh border. "Genuinely, I've tried it."

Harris had borrowed a map from a mate at the Rugby club.

According to the map the world ended at the Severn Bridge; England did not exist, and now they were lost.

"She's a better navigator than ewe," Harris said, referring to Cat who was dozing on the passenger seat, "even when she's sleeping."

Ed was wedged between the two of them with the gear stick between his legs.

The real reason they were lost was because, while it was free to cross either of the two Severn Bridges travelling in the English direction, you had to pay to enter Wales. Rightly so, no-one could argue with that. But Harris wanted to skip the toll, so they were taking a detour.

Talking seemed to help him. "Lucky it's only a train we're waiting for. In the days before the railways drovers would walk great 'erds of cattle from all over Wales and converge on the rich men's markets in the east…"

Ed assumed he was referring to London, not the Orient.

". . . they'd bring several 'undred cattle at a time, and flocks of sheep, pigs, *even* geese – a procession that could be 'alf-a-mile long. They travelled from dawn to dusk at two miles per 'our – didn't want to push the animals any faster in case they lost weight! Imagine getting stuck behind that lot, mayhem I bet! The noise of the animals, and the yappin' of the dogs, and the cries and shouts of the drovers…Turkeys! They also walked turkeys!"

There was a long pause. Ed went to say something but Harris raised a hand to silence him. "No, can't do it…" puffed Harris eventually. "It's enough to wreck ewer 'ead. Ewer the mind man – 'ow long would we be waiting by 'ere if there was 'alf-a-mile of animals movin' at two miles per 'our?"

It was well past closing time when they got home.

❖

It was a quiet week. Really. Harris and Cat were big into walking, so that's what the three of them did.

They walked the Taff Trail and returned to some favourite locations in the Black Mountains and, of course, had a long day on the beaches. Out of respect they always had to do the beaches.

The rest of the time, they just relaxed. Cat didn't seem to mind that Ed was around; she and Harris were tight, their relationship could stand most things.

WHEN HARRIS MET ED

LOOKING back, this was probably thirteen years ago, Ed and his friends deserved a good kicking. They were old enough to get served in pubs but too young to prove it. They dressed in affordable fashion and had their hair cut in the same salon as their mothers.

That Saturday they had been first in and last out of the pub. Now they were wobbling on a street corner under the neon light of a chip shop. They each had a polystyrene tray of chips in one hand and one of those wooden forky things in the other. The chips wore a wig of chemical-curry sauce. Ed's group were oblivious to the knot of lads across the street who hadn't drunk enough and hadn't had enough fun – yet. It was like sharks eyeing a few nursery fish who had drifted away from the school.

There was a rush of wind. In a flash Ed's mate Mike was on his arse wearing a polystyrene hat with a tear of curry sauce on his cheek and chips on his shoulder.

"What the ..!" he squeaked. "Oh shit," thought Ed in a deep voice.

"Are ewe fuckers taking the piss!" shouted the assailant who had six mates on the other side of the street; their knees were bent and testosterone revving - any sign of pride or resistance would be the green light for attack.

Mike was removing his polystyrene hat and wiping the worst of the sauce off his face and slowly getting up from the ground, careful to keep his hands close to his side. These boys had Valley accents, which meant they were fluent in fighting; where they come from even the nerdy kids would be brave enough to have a go. So when Ed's gang responded with complete, unmitigated humility it confused the hell out of the Valley Boys. They had never witnessed anything so pathetic as these posh, whiny girl-boys.

So it was. Without handing over any wallets or watches or girlfriends (because they didn't have any) they got away without a kicking.

When the Valley Boys felt their honour had been sufficiently honoured, they gave one final warning and one final reminder to Ed and his pals that they were the luckiest little fucks that ever lived, and walked off, like crows, down the street.

❖

Harris had brought his mam to Tenby. She wanted to go and he'd run out of excuses and here they were. They had a nice meal in the hotel and Harris had parked her back in her room. Then he went out for a bag of chips.

While his fish was cooking Harris pointed at things in the heated glass cabinet and ate them while he was waiting. A jumbo sausage, a pastie, a spring roll, another jumbo sausage, and so on…

There was some shouting on the street. He went to the window and watched while a gang of Valley Boys prepared to kick the shit out of a few surfers. The gang were looking for any small excuse, the surfers were doing their best not to give it to them. Any second now, thought Harris.

"Nine pounds and seventy pence," said the chip shop man.

"'Ere's a tenner, keep them warm, I'll be back."

The Valley Boys were walking up the street. Ed and Mike and Del and Pugh watched. They were in shock. How did they escape that?

A lad who could be their own age, but was definitely from another planet, came out of the chip shop. He ducked and turned to fit through the doorway.

" I 'ave seen all that through the window, bit cowardly of 'em, isn't it, seven on to four? 'Ows about I go and pummel the pigment out of them on ewer be-alf?"

Without waiting for permission, the Man Mountain took off in pursuit. Ed and his pals followed in his wake. The ground moved with each step he took. The Man Mountain passed under the archway in the fortified wall of the old town and paused. Looked left, looked right, let out a wild cry, and ran right.

When Ed rounded the corner, fifty yards ahead of him the Man Mountain was a windmill of arms and legs, and the Valley Boys were in little balls or flat shapes on the road. Ed stood there, mesmerised. His friends went in to the fray after the Mountain, a little bit like smoking the filter of a cigarette…

The Man Mountain went back to collect his fish supper. The lads made their way over to South Beach. Mike had a grazed fist because a prone figure had moved at the wrong moment and he'd hit a wall instead. Del was limping after stubbing his toe on a lamp-post. Pugh had a black eye because he'd gotten too close to the Man Mountain.

In those days the South Beach car park was on the beach. The boys rolled out their sleeping bags close to the cars and slept. Except for Ed, he'd forgotten his sleeping bag – how unlucky was that! He started off sleeping in the car but it was a warm summer night so he decided to lay out on the sand anyway.

Ed woke first, shivering. The sun was rising bright. He needed a piss. The beach was empty, but for some strange reason he decided to cross the dune and wee out of sight.

While urinating he saw a piece of plastic that could be a frisbee. Ed loved finding things. He liked saving money much more than spending it. He walked over to the brand new top-of-the-range Californian frisbee that turned out to be the lid of a mayonnaise tub.

He wandered back. Close to the brow of the dune he heard voices. The lads were waking up already – strange.

Lying on his stomach, looking through the dune grass, he watched two uniformed officers put his three friends in the back of a white squad car.

◆

Ed sat in the café with a hangover. Other than that he was alone. He had finished his fried breakfast and took sips of cold tea while looking out the window at the beach and harbour below.

Behind him he heard a voice he thought he recognised. He turned, it was the Man Mountain from last night, and an old lady with a large handbag.

"Ewe've got the best table," said the Mountain. "Mam likes a view, move over."

" 'ello Rory," said the old lady, sitting next to Ed. " 'Arris, ewe never said we was going to meet Rory, why didn't ewe tell me we was going to meet Rory?"

Harris, the Mountain, went to the counter. His mother smiled at Ed.

"Lovely day, init?" she said. She looked at his plate. Ed had mopped up all the sauces and juices with his last piece of toast. It was a very clean plate.

"The 'otel do a very nice breakfast buffette, it's nice when ewe can take what ewe want and as much as ewe like. Then we decided to come out for a walk and some fresh air."

She took her hearing aid out to clean it. Harris came back.

"Where to are ewer friends?"

Ed said how the police had collected them off the beach, how his bladder had saved him. His bladder and how he'd forgotten his sleeping bag. Harris looked sideways at Ed. "*Chwarae-teg* and fuck me, I like ewer style!"

" 'Arris Williams, mind ewer filthy language, will ewe?" Mrs Williams had re-loaded her hearing aid in time to catch that one.

"Sorry, Mam. How or-dacit is that though!" Harris was enthralled.

The waitress arrived with Harris's fry-up, a large pot of tea and a coffee for his mother. The waitress took Ed's plate and nearly had his tea mug too.

CAT'S STORY

AT midday Ed had received a telephone call at his parents house. It was Harris, they had been mates for maybe a year by this time. "Meet me at three on the point at Llantwit. Bring papers and a lighter."

At three Ed was on Llantwit Beach squatting in the shelter of a large rock enjoying his afternoon cigarette with the winter sun in his face and one eye on the car park so he didn't miss Harris.

The world went dark. Ed turned and Harris was standing there. He hardly recognised him; he had the look of a man who had arrived from a distant land on a home-made raft.

Harris coughed and from deep in his chest, somewhere near his waist, hawked up some tobacco and spat it onto the rock behind Ed's head. It looked like a bird's nest that had been flushed down the toilet.

"Lighter's fucked, papers are soaked so I've been chewin' it.

Tastes like shit, it doesn't kill ewe though."

Ed held out a hand with a freshly rolled cigarette and the lighter.

Harris took the cigarette, and the lighter, lit the cigarette and put the lighter back in Ed's still outstretched hand.

If Harris was small, he would probably be shivering, and this whole scene would be pitiful. But Harris was six-foot-four and eighteen stone. His dark mop of hair – long enough to curl, no longer – was plastered around his head and encrusted with sand and wisps of *Spirogyra*.

He was Neptune without a trident.

He'd started out in Barry. Ed looked back in that direction. There was no beach left. The waves were already breaking on Stout Point – known for the steepest, highest cliffs and the strongest currents. How the hell did he get round there? Ed shut his mouth. But it opened again. Jaysus.

Ed fished a can of coke out of a small pack of provisions. Harris downed it in two and gave a belch which reverberated off the cliff despite the strong wind.

There was a flash of amusement in Harris's eyes. No, wait, that was madness.

If you're nineteen years old and the only girl you will ever love breaks up with you, even though she never really loved you back anyway, well, that's Armageddon of the soul. That's a H-bomb in the heart. That's as shit as shit can be.

Teresa was not really Harris's girlfriend. No, she was. Or, at least, had been. But he had never really been her boyfriend. Teresa already had a boyfriend. Her real boyfriend played outside-half for Wales. Harris's position was somewhere in the middle, some of the time.

Harris loved rugby as much as he loved Wales. Which was a lot. He knew it was a serious infringement to break an International player's nose in the run-up to the Five Nations Championship, but he did it anyway. In front of Teresa. Who was not so secretly delighted that two men were breaking bones over her.

Now Teresa had decided she wanted to spend her life with a national hero rather than an apprentice mechanic. Her exact words were: "'Is nose will mend, ewer permanently fucked!"

Harris shouted back. "Well, ewer fucking loss!" She looked askance for a few moments then laughed a good laugh back at him. The kind that turns you to stone.

He'd acted out of anger, and so there would be consequences. He'd hit out. It was like smashing a mirror. Now he was faced with a thousand images of what he did not like.

He couldn't help it. Something came over him. That's women for you.

Now he was being penalised for ill discipline. Red carded. Cited. End of his career. Using rugby analogies helped him understand the seriousness of his situation.

The nicotine and sugar were not easing the situation. They were feeding it.

Harris took off again with Ed in pursuit.

If you drive fast enough on a rough road you ride over the bumps and skim over the pot-holes. It's a smooth ride. If you charge without fear over boulders and beach debris it's same as running on flat hard sand. The only problem is slowing down or stopping.

When Harris couldn't run any more he fell onto the wet sand. It was November, he was dressed in a T-shirt. In his head, in between the turmoil and vitriolic thoughts, occasionally, there was space, nothing, peace. Then he found second wind, leapt to his feet and ran on. As if his hair was on fire.

Harris leaned forward from his ankles; his head and upper body were travelling faster than his feet, his knees and elbows pumping like pistons. He crossed great swathes of the shoreline until he tripped or collapsed.

Ed would catch up while he heaved around on the ground. "Roll me another cigarette before I kill us both."

Harris was an aggregate of the five stages of grief, being held together by the same emotions that were tearing him apart. They were close to Monknash, and Harris was banging his head on the sand. He got to his feet, picked up a huge boulder and hurled it at the cliff, then narrowed his eyes to prepare for another charge, which is when he spotted the plastic bag in the shallows.

Harris picked it up and looked inside. At first they thought it was a rat. The drowned baby dog did not move. Maybe the mouth moved. Maybe. There was a weak cough.

Harris recognised a victim, a better victim than he would ever be. In an instant he transformed to compassionate protector. He placed the puppy inside his T-shirt.

It was easier to keep up with Harris now. It was a mile to Cwm Bach where they ran up the beach, crossed the stream, skipped the style and up the wibbly-wobbly path to The Seven Stars.

Harris walked casually into the pub and was greeted by men wearing T-shirts who had spent the day standing in fields and climbing telegraph poles and roofing houses. And there were some blonde, wispy looking characters dressed in pastel-coloured hoodies sitting in the dart-board corner sipping from bottles.

Harris roared over the heads of the workmen at the bar.

"Bardsley! I need a word and a pint and steak-and-ale pie and chips."

"In what order?

"Everything now."

There were only two people in the world who could talk to Bardsley like that: Scott Gibbs and Harris. Bardsley held the overview at The Seven Stars. It was a formidable task and Bardsley was formidable. He worked on the premise that if you want to control a bull, give it a big grazing field. All manner of shite could go down as long as it was within the field of play, which depended on Bardsley's mood. God help you if you crossed that line.

Bardsley barked orders at the kitchen, elbowed the bar boy into action, and directed Harris to the table by the fire.

"Is it true ewe broke Rory Quinnel's nose?"

"Look Bards, it wasn't my fault, it's a long story, I only. . ."

"'Ey, all's fair in love and war. Anyway, I like the look of Darren Evans. 'Opefully they'll give 'im a run-out, reckon that'll make a better 'alf-back partnership anyway. So my friend, what's the drama?"

Harris told him he had a poorly puppy in his shirt.

Bardsley's best friend was a dog and he didn't hesitate. "I know what we needs to do."

❖

The Seven Stars was a mile from a coastline exposed to the prevailing south-westerly winds and Atlantic swells where, on the dark days and stormy nights before the advent of modern navigation, ships looking for safe anchorage at Cardiff or Barry would be lured onto the lethal rock reefs and sand banks by the false lights of the infamous Wreckers of Wickham.

They say that the roof beams of the main building were salvaged from ships of the Spanish Armada, and that through the ages the bodies of drowned sailors were laid out in the corner, where the dart board was now, while the coffins were made next door. There was no end to stories of the ghosts and demons that terrorised previous generations of proprietors and clientele until, legends tell us, the last great Druid Queen of Wales – Megan the Wise – conducted a dramatic exorcism and peace was restored.

Still, nowadays, someone might say they have seen Amy

dressed in rags, walking the cellar stairs and serving tables, or Bernez the Sailor climbing the chimney. But usually that person has been drinking all day and happens to be alone at the moment when Amy or Bernez or one of the other phantom celebrities do their rounds. And then the previous summer, when it was busy, Bardsley complained that poltergeists were blocking the credit card machine – and on one occasion they even smashed the till! As far as Ed was concerned it was all good entertainment and being the *Scariest Pub in the World* certainly boosted the tourist trade.

❖

Harris was sitting next the fire, with the drowned puppy in his shirt. He was half way through his food. A knife and fork were still neatly wrapped up in a paper napkin on the table.

"'Ark at the steam coming off ewe," said Bardsley, momentarily distracted by the mist that surrounded Harris. "I know exactly what we need to do," he continued, focusing once more, "We need to invoke Megan the Wise. I'll give her a call."

Ed nearly spat a mouthful of beer over the pair of them. Bardsley looked at him for a moment, as if to say, "Shouldn't ewe be over in the dart-board corner with the rest of the waifs?" Bardsley got up to make the call.

Ed needed to settle himself. But, but, but...Megan the Wise was the mythical druid queen of a bygone age, she was not even real, and even if she was real she was dead already and she certainly did not have a telephone number.

Bardsley was back already. "Megan says I can bring ewe over in an 'our."

"An 'our!" protested Harris, spraying pie pastry across the table. "It could all be over. . ."

"Megan says an 'our," repeated Bardsley. "And just ewe and

the sorry creature. I mean the drowned one, not 'im," he added, pointing a thumb over his shoulder at Ed.

Ed missed the insult. He was thinking: if Megan really did exist maybe all the other bullshit was true too…

Harris belched loudly. It caught a few people off guard, including the bar boy who looked in the direction of the noise. Harris signalled another beer.

Ed wanted to meet Megan but he was also knackered. He liked the idea of another pint by the fire. The embers were glowing, and when you prodded it with the poker the sparks sparkled and the flames danced and the next chapter of the story appeared in his mind's eye.

Bardsley waited in the car.

Harris climbed the stone style and took a few small steps down the unlit path to a old wooden front door. As he lifted his fist to knock he heard the lock release and the door opened. There was no-one there. Just a flickering light at the end of the hall.

"This way," said a thin voice.

Harris could see bugger all. He had one hand holding the puppy against his chest, the other brushing the wall for reassurance, he edged down the passage. . .

"Stop there. Give me the being." Long fingers unfolded in his direction, took the lifeless dog and receded into the shadows.

Harris heard some deep exhalations and a few words, like singing or incantation. Something flashed momentarily, two diamantine eyes maybe? The hand appeared holding out the too-small dog now wrapped in white silk.

"It will live. . ." said Megan

Harris took the dog, mumbled a thank you, spun around and headed back down the hallway.

"Holding on to your anger is like holding a sword by the blade – you will only hurt yourself. Do not come back here."

Harris was grateful he had left the door open and that Bardsley was waiting with the car lights on.

◆

"Where's the dog?" said Ed when Harris finally returned.

"Stop aggravating the fire, will ewe!" said Harris, taking the poker out of Ed's hand. "She's with Bevan at the post office." He took a thirsty sup from his new pint. "My dog needs colostrum from a bitch. Colostrum 'as antibodies to protect against disease and deliver nutrients in a very concentrated low-volume form...and Bevan's spaniel 'as just 'ad pups."

Harris fell silent for a moment, reflecting on what had just happened. "I think I was expecting Megan to be like a crazy old witch or something, but she's a pensioner living in a semi-detached 'ouse near the main road. I couldn't go earlier because she was watching 'Coronation Street'. Then she couldn't find 'er glasses. I checked twice to make sure I was in the right 'ouse. She must be used to that, said people are often disappointed when she is not some kind of 'alf-mad gypsy, said that wisdom is actually very ordinary, said that in this age of tabloid newspapers it serves one not to display miracles. Said the dog was fine. Except the dog was not bloody fine. The dog 'ad to be dead. I watched 'er breathe life back into the dog. I'm calling my dog Cat. It's short for catatonia. Partly cos she was, and partly cos of Cerys Matthews."

Harris had completely forgotten he was the recently dumped pseudo-boyfriend of Teresa. Now he was a daddy.

◆

Two days later Harris picked Cat up from Bevan at the village post office. He took her home and fed her with water from a syringe every time she cried, which was about every three hours, day and night, for ages. Actually it was only a week, but if felt like ages. Then milk in drops from a syringe, then shoving her face in a bowl so she'd get the hang of it.

She was shitting blood for a few days so you can only imagine the celebration when she did a grown-up turd. Cat stayed real small for a real long time. She slept in an oven glove.

So it was. Cat was a dog that had an immaculate birth, manifesting out of a white plastic bag half-floating on the muddy waters of the Bristol Channel. That was all about twelve years ago. Cat was now fully grown. As fully grown as a Corgi can be.

LAND OF MY FATHERS

ED was running a marathon. Harris was reading a book. Difficult to say which was the more unlikely. The book was called *The Drover's Roads of Wales*.

During the week, on a walk, Ed made some comment about the inclement weather. Not a complaint, just conversation:

"Man up, why don't ewe?" snapped Harris with Cat at his heel. "It's not like we're going all the way to bloody England. Thank Christ! Them drovers who crossed these 'ills 'ad it colder, *and* the mist and rain. All they 'ad to wear was a long smock and trousers and knee-length woollen stockings – not gorrtext like 'ewe – and, if it was really bitter and piss wet they made leggings from brown paper, which they rubbed with soap to make it waterproof. Soap, mind ewe! And they used soap on the soles of the stockings, so that when the foot sweated it slid along the sock, instead of blistering against the wooden soles of the clog. Which, in-side-dentally, is a trick that was copied by 'Illary and Tenzin when they climbed Everest. Obvious really. Welsh technology gets mankind to the top of the world! Love it!"

Harris threw a stick into the larger of the two ponds under Beacon Hill.

"Fan-bloody-tastic dog that...every reason to be scared of water but she isn't. Y'know with the geese, before they set off for 'over there', the drovers marched 'em through a mixture of tar and sand which would 'arden into a protective covering for their feet. And the pigs 'ad little woollen socks with leather soles to make sure they arrived fit for slaughter. That's thoughtful, init?"

He added after a few moments of silent thought: "Cat and I were going to go vegetarian, but the vet discouraged it."

A few moments later…

"I was thinking about T'resa the other day. . ."

Ah shite. It had all been going so well. Ed braced himself for a barrage of vengeance and vitriol.

". . .and I realised that if she 'adn't left me and gone on to 'ave two failed marriages and a brood of brats, me and Cat would never 'ave met."

His dog had returned a stick that was twice as big as she was. "Good girl, Cat."

You would have to know Harris, and more of the story, to understand why that comment stunned Ed. If Harris could get over Teresa, world peace was only a matter of time.

But he wasn't finished. "And I 'ave been thinking about the bastard who threw Cat in the sea. I am glad my campaign to find the fucker failed. Because I would 'ave killed him and it would 'ave been public cos his DNA would 'ave been spattered across the principality, and I would be doing time with my brother and 'alf the rest of my school class. So I am glad ee evaded me. Because what I am concluding is, see, no-one is born that evil, just sometimes we get twisted by difficult circumstances and adverse conditions, and without the right support we can descend into acting like a wild beast. Like T'resa. Or the bastard that put Cat in a binbag and lobbed 'er into the sea. His parents probably put 'im out with the rubbish when ee was a kid. So, I 'ave made my peace. Don't get me wrong, if I ever bumped into 'im I would still throw 'im off the cliff with a fertiliser bag duck-taped over 'is 'ead. The difference now is, I would make sure it was 'igh tide. And I would call the Coastguard, after a while, maybe 'alf way through my third pint."

Holy shit! Something or someone was having a disturbingly positive influence on Harris. If he continued on this trajectory he'd start sprouting angel wings.

Ah no. . .he'd have to forgive England first. . .and that would never happen.

❖

Harris was generally happy. And he was especially happy when Wales beat England in rugby. But all the rest of the time he was just *generally happy* − because all the rest of the time Wales were in between beating England in the rugby.

Until he went to Bristol Airport to pick up Ed, Harris had never been abroad. Except to Twickenham for rugby. And once to Wembley.

The *once* was in '99, when the Millennium Stadium was under construction and Wales played their home games in the temporary principality of Wembley Stadium − not the new fancy washing-up bowl Wembley, the old one, with two towers, like it was a fortress.

Rugby is no ordinary game and this was no ordinary game of rugby.

The English team came out onto the pitch first, but even though the pitch was in London, you could hear "Calon Lân" being sung over the English cheering. There was "God Save the Queen" swiftly followed by "Hen Wlad Fy Nhadau" − *Land of My Fathers* - with Max Boyce *and* Tom Jones at the microphone. Such a day is seared on your heart forever.

England are winning, until four minutes into injury-time when Scott Gibbs, running from fifty yards out and evading the tackles of half the English back-line, scores the try. But, still, in order to take the Grand Slam away from England, Neil Jenkins has to make the conversion. He has already been named Man of the Match. . .He kicked it! Of course he did! Jenkins kicked 8 from 8 (again) that day. . .But the referee doesn't blow-up, he allows the English to re-start – it isn't over yet. From the kick-off England press into the Welsh half and are awarded a scrum on the twenty-five yard line. The ball comes back for an attempted drop goal. It is wide.

It is w - i – d – e !

And Harris was by the tunnel and he could see how, a few minutes before, the lads who had been putting the English colours on the Five Nations Trophy were now having to take them off again – because England had not only lost the game but the Grand Slam, and Scotland would win the Championship on points difference.

Harris nearly died of pride.

Really. He was only saved by the prompt action of paramedics.

"They were taking all the measurements and telling me to calm my breathing. Thing is, ewe can't sing with an oxygen mask over ewer face. The whole world was singing, I wanted to sing. I needed to sing! I'd rather die than not sing, but obviously the medics 'ad to put my well-being first. Lucky for me one of 'em was married to a girl from Tongwynlais so ee 'ad a proper grasp on the gravity of the situation and removed the mask for the chorus. If *Sosban Fach* were the last words I ever coughed I wouldn't be sorry, who would be?

"There were a few of us in the 'ospital that evening, we'd all 'ad near-death experiences of one kind or another. We were all put up one end of the ward. We done some more singing that evening.

"We sang 'Calon Lân' and, out of compassion, translated it for the nurses:

I don't ask for a luxurious life,
the world's gold or its fine pearls,
I ask for a happy heart,
an honest heart, a pure heart…

"Of course, we sang 'Arglwydd, arwain trwy'r anialwch', that's 'Bread of 'Eaven' to you:"

I am weak, but thou art mighty;
Hold me with thy powerful hand:
Bread of heaven, bread of heaven
Feed me till I want no more.
Feed me till I want noooo more. . .

❖

Whenever Ed went back to Wales he made sure he had at least one day walking the beaches. Of course Harris and Cat came too. Of course.

"The Corgis kept the 'erd together, low to the ground, they would snap at their 'eels while avoiding the kicks," said Harris

Ah so! Now it made sense. This whole drover fascination was Harris doing research on Cat's back-story.

"They found their own way 'ome, all the way from London, mind ewe. When the dogs arrived the wives knew the men were only a few days behind."

This coast had vertical cliffs of layer-cake rock that would go orange in the setting winter sun. Not this day though. As they reached the point near Cwm Bach the light was fading and the weather was closing in.

"C'mon," said Harris, "ewe can't shear a wet sheep. Scott Gibbs was 'aving a pint in The Stars last time I was in there."

He lead the way up the wibbly-wobbly path singing "Bread of Heaven". Cat yapped. Dogs were allowed in The Stars, in fact they were celebrated. None more so than Cat, the dog that local legend said had a miraculous birth on this very beach.

◆

From when he was young Ed believed he would find a vast treasure that would change his life forever. Some days, especially when he was troubled, walking beneath the cliffs of the Heritage Coast, rounding those headlands that tried in vain to delay the coursing tide, he would actively look for it.

There had been that many ship wrecks on these beaches, *anything* really was possible.

The treasure was never going to be a sea-chest of Spanish gold, not wealth in that way, even the little boy knew that. Knowledge was riches; it would be a message in a bottle or a map. But most likely a book.

Cardiff had old shopping malls called "Arcades", the walkways paved with immense flagstones, the window frames ornate and wooden. The shops were quirky; it could take some time to work out what they were selling. Ed's favourite were the second-hand bookshops; maybe today he would find The Book?

He found a café up some stairs at the back of a church smack in the centre of town. He had his custard slice with a cup of tea there. Everyday of his holiday he had a custard slice. Always with a cup of tea.

Downstairs he sat in a pew. This church still had atmosphere; Ed sat there flying an imaginary kite in a pristine sky for a few minutes, connected to the present moment through awareness of his breathing. It was a real buzz to be in a sacred silence in the middle of a busy city.

Streaky had said something about "stillness in the movement". Ed had thought he meant something like pushing a pause button. Freeze the action. Stop the world. Have a break. Then hit the play button again.

Those words exactly fitted with where he was.

Here, now.

He witnessed the buzz all around him from a quiet place.

All pervading peace in the heart of the principality.

He loved Wales.

What he was loving more was a feeling of home inside of himself, a feeling that he had never experienced here, or anywhere else. Streaky says it's innate, portable.

He felt so spacious he was worried people would notice. He got up self-consciously and bought some charity Christmas cards he knew he would never send.

MARATHON

TWIN sisters passed him. He was at mile fourteen of his first real marathon.

"Great form!" the girls said as they glided by.

Great form! No-one had ever said that to him. Maybe they meant Streaky, but they were definitely looking at him.

No-one had ever said that to him even when he thought he was exhibiting great form. Especially then. It's a surprising life.

It seemed "natural" was what got you noticed. It was somewhere about now Ed came up with the phrase, "If you are not smiling, it's not natural."

At least he was finally warm.

The evening before he had released Mr Blanco from incarceration in the long-term car park at the airport and driven west for an hour to the car park of a beach hotel where the starting line was.

He had raided Mr B's pantry and cooked himself a whole packet of pasta with a jar of pesto rosso, half a block of cheese and a full pot of tea. He was so full, movement was difficult, but he managed to set up the bed and fit into his sleeping bag.

It was 9.30pm on marathon eve and ice was already starting to form on the inside of the windows. The sky was clear, the stars were out.

Two hours later he was still awake and getting cold. He found a picnic blanket with a silver-foil lining in the gas canister cupboard and laid it out over his summer-weight sleeping bag. By midnight he was warm but getting wet from all the moisture condensing on the silver.

This could be a chance to try that exercise that the woman at the dog shelter had told Harris about.

"It's quite versatile," Harris had said, "It's a remedy for being miserable and feeling sorry for ewerself. When facing difficulties it stops ewe being so self-absorbed. And I punch people less. What I never really realised before was, 'ow much time we spend comparing ourselves with others. And usually we focus on people who are doing better than us, who 'ave what we want. And so she was telling me to open my eyes, see the whole picture, while there are some who 'ave more than me, comparing myself to them is only going to make me depressed and resentful. If I want to feel lucky, to count my blessings, I should remember the people who have nothing – the people who, if they 'ad what I 'ad, would feel like lottery winners. 'Oh,' she said, 'by the way,' she said, 'those that 'ave what ewe want, they still don't 'ave what *they* want.'"

At the time Ed hadn't understood that, but now he thought he did. Wherever we are it will always be possible for us to identify people more fortunate than ourselves, and people less fortunate than ourselves. Ed had nothing to lose, which was a good starting point; he would give it a go.

So, instead of thinking about himself in relation to all the other runners, "the competition", in their warm homes or in the hotel walking barefoot on their thick bedroom carpets after a hot shower, relaxing into a bed that is too big for them and letting the extra duvet and pillows slide off onto the floor – instead of that, he would think of himself in relation to people sleeping on the street, not just tonight, but every night. He remembered reading a newspaper article where this guy said sleeping rough was easy compared to thinking about how he came to be there.

Ed felt luckier. As he breathed in he empathised with their misfortune, as best he could imagine it. And as the fine mist of his exhalation dispersed he shared with them his good fortune, like choosing to be where he was. And a pasta supper, a strong pot of tea, and a soft bed.

After a few more breaths he had some insight into the difference between himself and a homeless person. Not so much. It's wafer thin. It's just circumstances.

He thought about hungry people. And sick people.

And on Marathon Eve he thought about people of all ages who would be delighted if they could just walk themselves down to the corner shop or climb a flight of stairs.

He thought about all those people who didn't have a passion, a reason to get out of bed in the morning. He still could not sleep but he felt lucky. Nothing had changed except his mind.

❖

It was not the morning, the early hours just. He got out of the sleeping bag, he was already dressed, hat and all. He shivered up to the hotel, tried the door, and went back to the van. Still feeling lucky-ish.

He put on the stove, and while the water boiled he put some oats, honey and raisins in a soup flask. And a tea-bag in a thermal mug.

He poured boiling water over both, placed the lids on quickly and made a mental note that hot-water bottles were not just for old ladies and that he must add one to the Mr B inventory.

After fifteen minutes he opened the flask, hot steam rose off the porridge and he spooned it into himself. The tea was nectar.

At this time of year, piss-wet and blowing-a-gale would be the norm. The freezing weather was good news. The sky was clear, the night was still, it would be a fine day.

As the crowd gathered Ed got super-psyched. Over-psyched. At registration he asked a marshal at what point you turned off if you wanted to just do the half-marathon. She looked at the colour of his number.

"You signed up for a marathon, so do it."

Instead of making him feel resolute and determined, she made him feel scared.

You could travel around the world and get up to all kinds of crazy stuff and still be a baby.

That's when he saw Streaky approaching.

Streaky listened to Ed's story, how cold he was, but he couldn't understand why Ed hadn't just gone for a run on the beach. "It's beautiful hard sand as far as the eye can see. I'm not going to wet-nurse you all the way round. First you need to believe this is within your power, and you will likely find it so."

They were bunched up behind the start line. When it came to running Streaky was not used to all this standing around but it didn't faze him, he looked the same as always – warm, relaxed, happy.

"Outer appearance is only half the story, less than half the story…look at us all," he said.

Ed looked around. People of all shapes and sizes, powers and graces, chatting or gazing into the distance, in balanced equipoise or skipping from one foot to the other. Ed was bobbing up and down, wringing his hands and hugging himself. He was pale blue.

"…what ultimately determines how we perform is how our mind is, our physical body can only bring us so far. It's the same in life, we usually spend all our time and most of our energy concerned with our look, how we appear to others, our wardrobe, the car we drive, the plaque on the door.

"The emphasis is always on the object, the result, what we are looking at rather than on our mind and *how we are seeing*. Beauty is in the eye, and the mind, of the beholder. Our finishing time is not important, what is important is the mind of the person who finishes."

Right now Ed was only interested in what he was not wearing, and how much longer it would be before they could start running. If Tough-Lady Marshal marched over now and shot him with the starter gun at least he wouldn't be cold any more.

Tough-Lady Marshal and her colleagues did well to get everyone on the seaside of the start line, and the road clear of cars, just twenty minutes later than the scheduled start time.

The winter sun was rising over the hotel roof and ready to start shining on everyone.

Ed was blue, busting for a wee and trying to snuggle up to people without it being too obvious.

There was a minute of silence for a member of the local running club who had passed away earlier that week. Then they sang the Irish anthem. A stirring tune with many verses. Everyone bounced up at down ready for the off, but next there would be a blessing.

An elderly priest was helped to his feet and given a microphone. He took a moment to savour the atmosphere and another moment to consider the blessing.

"For Christ's sake…" started someone behind Ed.

The priest said something, a hooter sounded, and they were off – or the people at the front were anyhow.

All that was history. He was at mile fourteen already and feeling strong. He had Streaky to thank for that; he kept saying, "Start slow, go slower."

So Ed was warm. And the "great form" comment from the fit ladies was a perfect bonus.

He was hoping Tough-lady Marshal would be at the finish line to see him with his hands raised and smiling, tired but triumphant.

Things change. By the eighteen mile mark Ed had been dropped by those runners who would finish comfortably. He was a straggler.

Streaky had promised they would run together. And at the beginning it had been fun – Streaky could talk, even going up hills and was all hoppy'n'skippy – but as time went on and he was still talking and and bouncing it was starting to get more than annoying.

"The beauty of the marathon is, its twenty-six-and-a-bit miles. You know that so you can pace yourself. So many things in life are a mystery, but with the marathon you always know where it ends."

"Run on," pleaded Ed again. "I'll see you at the end."

This time Streaky listened.

His parting advice was, "Tickle your heart with your beard", and he set off like a delinquent greyhound just escaped from his kennel.

Ed waited till he was probably out of earshot then called up the road after him, "Tickle your own fecking heart with your own fecking beard!"

"Are you alright fella?" said a Dublin accent close by. Ed nodded.

At twenty miles Ed was all alone, in a world of his own and being punished.

Strong at mile fourteen was good – but only if "Strong At Mile Fourteen" was his goal. Otherwise it didn't mean shit.

To finish is his goal. He can change his goal.

Does he want to?

Ed could give up. Giving up is not dramatically collapsing

into the hedge. It can be a very private thing. Sometimes in his life Ed had given up without anybody else knowing. He knew giving up does not mean stopping. It's when his heart looks elsewhere, or when a micro-switch in his head says, "I'll not give it My Everything, I'll just go through the motions. . ."

He weighed up that option and was relieved to discover he did care. Very much.

There was a pain in his chest. It could be heart-burn or a stitch. He could be seconds away from a heart attack. How would he know? It, dying, could be that easy.

It had to be simple; it's the only thing in the world everyone can do! He smiled a cynical smile.

If he knew when he would die, would he live a better life? Would he pace himself then?

Now elderly people were overtaking him. He thought he recognised the priest who gave the blessing.

"He who would be first shall be last! Haha!"

Several years before he had found a book in a Cardiff arcade called *The Seven Storey Mountain,* thinking at first it might be about heli-snowboarding in Alaska.

Actually it was written by Thomas Merton who was a Trappist monk and a mystic and had never been snowboarding in his life. Ed particularly liked one quote, *Souls are like athletes that need opponents worthy of them if they are to be tried and extended and pushed to the full use of their powers, and rewarded according to their capacity.*

He was thinking about Merton's quote when the cramp started. But he did not give up and he was rewarded with a second highlight of the day.

Heading down the beach road to the finish line, finishers and their families were walking back down the course to find their cars, and stopping to cheer the stragglers.

One old lady clapped her hands. "Well done, well done…

Jaysus!" She turned to her family. "He's run all that way in flip-flops... Well done!"

Streaky put a cup of sugar-tea in his hands, held his shoulders and directed him to a line of massage tables manned by trainee therapists giving complimentary treatments.

◆

Streaky accepted Ed's offer of a lift back to the Beara Peninsula.

Ed hobbled in the direction of the car park and temporarily forgot his discomfort when Mr Blanco came into view. Mr B was head and shoulders above every car in any car park.

"It's like no other car you will ever drive. It's not a car for a start." Ed levered himself up onto the driver's seat and lifted his legs in one at a time, placing them near the pedals. He adjusted the seat to have himself more upright, and lowered the arm rests, and shut the door and put the seat belt on. He turned the key a single click and sat there in silence.

"I need to wait for this orange engine light to go off, the battery is good but still takes about thirty seconds. He's vintage..."

They sat there in silence for half-a-minute before the light went off and Ed turned the key another click and the engine rumbled into wakefulness.

"Like it," said Streaky. "That gave us time to appreciate how a collection of unrelated inanimate objects and liquids, assembled together, carefully tuned, can become a living system! And it is now about to propel us – and all the other bits'n'pieces that complete what you call Mr Blanco – up the road in perfect choreography."

He was still hoppy'n'skippy but Ed could cope with it now. Despite the exhaustion, he was feeling a good bit of accomplishment himself.

Down the road and Streaky's tone changed. "The problem with friends is that they like you the way you are."

Ed looked across at him. "And?"

"Friends like you the way you are, *and yet*, everyone I've ever met wants to change."

Ed said nothing.

"So in that case, a real friend is the one who helps you change, who shows you your blind spots, removes your edges."

Ed had to respond. "Sounds like you are warming up to giving me some advice…"

"What I am saying is you've been running a couple of months, and it was refreshing, re-vitalising *and* relaxing. It has taken the lid off your neurosis. But needing to run a marathon, and now running the marathon, you just turned it into something else, like you always do. Maybe it's about adequacy or validity but you're back at square one.

"Dr George Sheehan wrote a great book, it's on the shelf back at the cabin, *Running and Being*. The clue is in the title. Homage to Doc George! He wrote something like, *If you run enough, you come to know, that the smallest divisible unit is the universe.*

"If you run enough in the right way it becomes a communion with the road, with the nature and with yourself. It's difficult to say where you end and the running begins. The sun, the wind and the rain, and the grass you run on, and the air you breathe.

". . . the universe *is* the smallest divisible particle. That's holistic. Real holistic. As in w-h-o-l-e-istic. If you want a running goal, don't make it 26.2 miles, make it that. Running and Being. You want to give it a go? We'll need to adjust your focal setting. Are you up for this?"

"I don't know."

"Good answer. You absolutely don't know. Question is, do you want to find out?"

◆

They stopped at Ballylickey Emporium for an espresso. And organic fizzy drink, olives and 100 grammes of sliced salami, and oat cakes and cottage cheese with crisps and spelt baguettes.

Both tables inside the cafe were taken so they retired with their picnic to Mr B.

It took a while, what with the getting out of Mr B and the getting back in, and he had to park nearly ten metres from the door because it was Saturday and the car park was full, but the walk did him good. In fact another hour of driving and his hips may have seized forever.

The food intake changed the energy. Streaky got on a bit of a roll. "When we talk about change, there are two types of change. One is shuffling a deck of cards, moving things around to create a more comfortable constellation. That's pseudo-change. The other is more fundamental. *Real change.* You have eyes but you don't see! You need to zoom out to take a closer look. You've gotta change your focal setting!"

Ed was shovelling food into his mouth while he listened.

"It's like you have created a parallel universe. You occupy the same space, and the same time, but you live in unawareness. It's like the first day I was saying…the contradiction."

Streaky left another pause, time for Ed to chew on it.

"Look. Look! First *out* of the window. Then *in* the window. Next *at* the window. You can see *through* the window, or see the reflection *in* the window or the window itself."

Ed saw the Emporium at the end of the car park. And himself in the window. And he saw the glass.

"This is just an example. An example of 'what we see is determined by how we look'. We decide where to put our focus. We need to change your focal setting. This is not just an exercise, it is how the world is. And how we see. Or don't see."

It was over. No, not quite.

"Don't wait till it's too late."

Back on the road in a twenty-five-year-old van. Going up hill, turning left, the fuel gauge can read quarter of a tank; moments later, downhill and turning right, the needle points to half. Ed pointed it out to Streaky.

"Ah the joys of it! Just like running, no?"

Ed himself was running on vapour. He talked to stay alert enough to drive. "How to get a handle on it all. That's where I struggle. And I am not alone."

He told Streaky how he had been hanging out for something better and working himself up into a state about it. "I've read some stuff on science of the mind, consciousness, supernature and chaos theory, the mystery of time and space...and the travelogues of Chatwin, Hesse, Kerouac and the like...they knew it was out there, but I don't think they found it."

"They did and they didn't. And Robert Pirsig too," said Streaky, "Don't forget him. He said, *The place to improve the world is first in one's heart and head and hands, and then work outward from there.* The running has got you now. It's in your blood. You have tasted the freedom. You are a rat up a drainpipe, there is no turning back.

You have run some of the restlessness out of you. Now you have to begin again. More intelligently."

On the stereo:

I hurt myself today
to see if I still feel.
I focussed on the pain
the only thing that's real.

You gotta love Johnny Cash.

5

UNLOCKING THE UNIVERSE

ED was holding the anatomy and physiology book that Streaky had recommended. There was one of his yellow book marks in the opening pages: *In an ever-changing world we are looking for a perfect scenario. We are looking for a perfect scenario in a world that is ever-changing. Good luck!*

It was the day after the marathon. Ed had no injuries as such, but he was sore and aching and wasted. And happy to sit in a chair with books.

Streaky had talked about change: "To change, the first thing you have to do is recognise change – to see change, how nothing stays the same in you and in the world around you. Everything is impermanent and everything is interdependent. For example, describe running to me, what is running?"

Ed hesitated. "Well…moving one foot in front of the other as fast as you can…well, quickly…it's the fastest . . ."

"Yep. Okay. Now read the anatomy and physiology book. Then describe running."

❧

The bookmark had been at the start of the chapter on the skeletal system. If Ed was to describe running it made sense to begin with bones and muscles. *The skeletal system is a framework of 206 bones that support and protect the muscles and the organs…*but he was quickly out of his depth, flicking back and forth between the pages and paragraphs. The book was arranged in chapters, one for each system, but the systems were inseparable – totally interdependent. Nothing happened in isolation.

For example, movement happens when a nerve impulse (of the nervous system) contracts the muscles (of the muscular system) that bridge the bone joints (of the skeletal system), so creating leverage. Meanwhile the digestive system breaks down foodstuffs into nutrients which are transported to bone tissues by the circulatory system. The red blood cells of the circulatory system are manufactured in the bone marrow. Bone marrow production is stimulated by the kidneys of the urinary system. It goes on . . .

He never made it to the second half of the book – the endocrine, lymphatic, reproductive, respiratory and urinary systems – yet he was sure they were something to do with running too.

He was in the middle of an anatomy and physiology epiphany, and feeling lucky that anatomy and physiology books didn't talk about psychological, emotional or subtle energy systems. He promised himself that from now on, instead of being surprised and disappointed when he was tired, injured or ill, he would be amazed when he was strong and healthy.

❖

Exhausted by the marathon, which he hadn't properly prepared for, Ed got a serious dose of man flu. His habit, which he did not resist, was to be surprised and disappointed.

He couldn't run and he thought like his life was over. Grow up!

Did he really want to be happy? He seemed to spend more time looking for excuses to be miserable.

He reminded himself of his promise. And that all it took was for a few tiny cells of the tissues of one organ in one system to misbehave and the whole human organism crashed. He was only as strong as his weakest part. Everything was at the mercy of everything else. Interdependence. All this is happening inside of him all the time, night and day, at rest or play?

And, zooming out, human beings were a single, tiny cell in the great organism called the universe! Holy guacamole! When all humans beings played their part there was harmony, when they misbehaved there was conflict, wars. There are consequences. Cause and effect.

Once we see movement and change we see life!

❖

Once we see movement and change we see life is what he thought when he was in a good mood. When he was in a bad mood it became, *If everything is always changing, why bother?* Why bother being fit, going to work or helping out a neighbour? Why bother building all these sandcastles?

He had to wait for a good mood for the answer. When the good mood came the answer was worth waiting for.

The answer was *because* everything changes. That's why bother!

Because everything changes he has the power, the possibility, the opportunity to influence the change. He was not stuck in a rut, he could change the world. Even a small change to a minor cause or condition could have a big impact on the whole. Impermanence and interdependence were the power. And the hope.

Things clearly existed, they were not "nothing", but they were not permanent or solid either – because they change. And every object and circumstance – including him – was the result of multiple causes and conditions.

❖

Why was he running? This seemed a good time to ask himself that question. If he didn't know why he was doing something, how would he know accomplishment or success?

The marathon had been his goal. He had been focused and

clear. He had pushed himself daily to extend his limits. He didn't have a rest day when he felt off-colour, and he didn't stop when he was tired.

He had gone beyond "good health" and into "peak fitness". He had made it. He was there. What was the view like from here? Good while it lasted. But a nervy, unstable place. Balancing somewhere between personal best and over-use injuries.

Is that what he wanted? A few months of peak performance and then a crash-and-burn muscle-pull or flu that kept him off the trails for weeks, or longer?

He had run beyond health and well-being. It was like climbing Everest. He had run the marathon *because it is there.*

He remembered the night he posted his marathon entry. He didn't want to drink his life away, or run himself into a heart attack. There had to be a middle way.

Maybe once he had answered *Why am I running?* he could ask himself the *Why am I living?* question.

❖

For the following week when Ed went outside he wore boots and a lot of clothes and just walked. As he walked he was aware of his breathing. When he was too dreamy he grounded himself with some flesh-and-bone detail: oxygen pathways, and all the levers and pendulums. When the detail became overwhelming he just considered the body as a mass of cells, because the cell was the smallest unit of matter that could live independently and reproduce itself. Cells were made of molecules built of atoms. Atoms were as tiny as you could go. And atoms were empty except for light and energy. Thinking of himself as a mass of cells made of energy and light helped him relax and be spacious.

When he relaxed too much and started to space out, he remembered he was walking and wondered again at the anatomy-and-physiology genius of it all.

He oscillated between the extremes of empty-except-for-light-and-energy and human embodiment, reminding himself that both were true and did not contradict each other; how amazing that was.

Maybe when he understood how that could be possible he would be able to decipher the next of Streaky's anatomy and physiology bookmarks:

Surfaces still appear as such, but maybe less solid, more transparent, there can be a space where we never saw space before. It will reflect the degree of your own relaxation. In stagnant and oppressive conditions we can see movement, lightness. Our seeing is opening, there is more balance and harmony in our lives and in the world.

A growing tree does not change space.

Ed looked at the mountain. He visualised the complex underground network of mine shafts and passageways permeating in all directions, to all depths, even under the sea, a giant honeycomb linking vast and silent caverns, like empty churches.

He found out that 300,000 tonnes of ore had been shipped from this beach to Swansea for smelting.

Swansea was in south Wales. Ed went to university in Swansea. He studied geology and oceanography because geology had been fun in school and he liked surfing. Three years later he left with a degree and the knowledge that geology had been fun in school and he liked surfing. It was not a complete waste of time though; he did meet the people who told him about the rafting in Nepal, and the ski-tech jobs in Austria and the field station in the Bahamas.

Anyway, any graduate of schoolboy geology would know that to access and extract 300,000 tonnes of productive ore, it would be necessary to remove perhaps fifty times that volume. What'd that be? Fifty times three-hundred thousand...That'd be…that'd be fifteen million tonnes of rock removed to produce that much ore! Fifteen million tonnes of rock with dynamite and picks and shovels and steam engines. And candles!

That was amazing, but what was more amazing to Ed was that while it looked big and solid, there were actually fifteen million tonnes of rock missing from the middle of this mountain; it was not as solid as it seemed. When he looked a little deeper he saw nothing was quite as solid as it seemed.

◆

Ed had read that a single living cell carried all the necessary information to construct the complete organism. He was wondering if there was a kernel of wisdom that answered every question. He intuited there was. And this was the wisdom he had been searching for since childhood.

Ed lived in a world of wonders, yet managed to make everything banal and mundane; he was surrounded by surprises which came one on top of another and yet he didn't notice any of them. Despite the truth of impermanence and regardless of ubiquitous interdependence, Ed only woke up a little when things were very pleasant. Or very unpleasant. His modus operandi was sleep, was indifference.

Elie Wiesel said:

> *The opposite of love is not hate, it's indifference.*
> *The opposite of art is not ugliness, it's indifference.*
> *The opposite of faith is not heresy, it's indifference.*
> *And the opposite of life is not death, it's indifference.*

All the "normal" things he barely noticed, he did not even know they were happening…Indifference was like a lethal injection, it robbed him of life!

Ed made the conscious decision to be more curious, more engaged. He could be like a child from a landlocked city who sees the sand and the ocean for the first time. That attention and that wonder.

❖

Ed was enjoying the challenge. Running without shoes was tough on him. Can't go out if you are low, or ill, or with food in your stomach – can't get too cold, or too tired. Can't be sloppy about it. The movement needs awareness. Can't coast down a hill with your mind elsewhere like you can on a bike. Or ease off and let the wind carry you while taking a slurp from a drink bottle. It was a high-maintenance relationship, which is why it felt so good when it was going well. Until this week he never even knew he had a rectus femoris. Now he knew he had two.

❖

Through time, the pressure points shifted as he ran. It began with the calves, the Achilles, the hips, the top of the foot. And now it was the ankles. This is a process that happened over months, and it happened each time he went for a run. Each time he detected a niggle, he adjusted his form or found a new loosening stretch or massage. He was constantly making changes and moving to the next level.

That was the point. He was not looking at pain, discomfort, failure. He could see it all as movement. And change. And progress, which some days was backwards.

❖

Lungs and oxygen were Ed's favourite. It never got boring. We breathe into our lungs, but our lungs are not plastic shopping bags, we don't just breathe it all out again. The fresh air is somehow absorbed into the blood, and…and . . .now breathe in, and out, and tell me that's not an amazing thing to be happening inside of you every second of every day. And night.

And then our partners the trees, who take our *used air* and make it new again.

Thank you for that now.

He was beginning to see his body as much more ephemeral, an ongoing coalescence in a dance with dissipation. That birth and death were not the bookends of something solid.

He was on a kind of natural high and starting writing bad poetry. And thinking psychedelic thoughts: When does one run end and the next one begin?

My meal is part of my next run. And my sleep, and washing my kit, and cutting my nails. Even calling my parents. This breath. My next thought. Nothing is separate.

I am either running, or warming up, or warming down. Its the thread that flows through every aspect of how I live each day. There's the period where you are just looking forward to running. The bit before you get changed and warmed up. And afterwards is rest and recovery. It is the before and after without which there would be no running.

◆

The flower grows without mistakes. A man must grow himself until he understands the intelligence of a flower. Ed had read that in a book of Buddhist sayings in a dentist's waiting room. He had looked up from the book. There were no flowers, just a tank of goldfish swimming in circles.

He found himself staring at trees, looking for help. Mmm.

Help was forthcoming. The leaves would come in spring when the wind and rain eased, and the sun shone, and nutrients in the soil awoke and were drawn up through the roots, into the trunk and along the branches. In fact, the tree received so much help in being a tree it hardly seemed fair to separate it from the rest of the natural world. There was a oneness there. A oneness that did not detract from the tree but added wonder and specialness to it.

There was intelligence in standing your ground and receiving what you were given and giving what you can. With grace and beauty.

Running and being, Ed decided, must be when we were out running, and we were very present, and we understood and felt that we were a part of the universal drama.

In the following days he saw lots of intelligence: bright yellow daisies growing on the wind-blasted sand dune and clever sea pink in cracks of the cliff. He ran on smiling.

He felt he was ready to come back to *A growing tree does not change space*. Mmm. Well, if everything, ultimately, was energy and light maybe that made sense too. Maybe.

He remembered what Streaky said about growing up; it had been in a different context but it felt relevant all the same. He said, "How we lived then, inside and outside was less clear, it was all the same place…".

The outer environment is important but not more important than the inner environment. In fact it was difficult or even impossible to draw a line, to separate them.

❖

Ed needed an excuse to take care of himself, to shop, cook and eat mindfully.

If he wanted to be strong and healthy and run a long run he had to support that aspiration through his lifestyle; he was really seeing *what you put in is what you get out*. He was really seeing what a wonderfully resourceful and weakly dependant entity our bodies were.

Sitting on a sofa all day requires no discipline – anything goes.

By living a simple and active life he was becoming much more aware of the cause-and-effect laws his body lived by.

❖

Ed stopped to check he had it right. He had it right. He was amazed. Without trying, he had given up alcohol and cigarettes. It was an accident; he hadn't meant to. Giving up drink and fags had never occurred to him because it was such a big part of his life. Wow! You don't have to stop anything, just start new things and the old stuff will get left behind, gather dust, become obsolete.

On a clear day he could see the ancient monastic isle of Sceilig Mhichíl, a dot in the Atlantic, sailing away to America, and that's when he understood how it could happen.

The first step to being a saint would be to put some distance between yourself and distraction, and non-virtue. Not so much working hard at being good, just giving your goodness space to manifest. But how brave! What belief and courage! To live in the middle of an infinite ocean, at the mercy of elements. Ed was in awe, until he realised that was the perfect description of his recent past.

Maybe if you have put your faith and trust in non-sense for long enough, living on an island in the Atlantic is the natural next step . . .

Not bravery but necessity. The world asks so many difficult questions of us. We can keep saying "Pass", or we can try to give an answer.

BLOC MÓR

AT the top of the cliff, along a hedge of fuchsia, willow and brambles and wire, Ed found a gap, a path into a wood of low, wind-bent trees stationed in thin soil. The slope fell away steeply, the path twisted back and forth; he stepped over fallen trees and broken branches.

At the apex of each bend there was a pile of cut branches. He emerged out of the trees and just fifty feet below him was the pulsating tide. Close enough to touch. He would touch it.

He slid the last piece on his feet and butt and hands.

Many years ago this steep cliff had collapsed and collapsed

again and become this wooded valley. The angular boulders were the size of cars and lorries and garden sheds. He scrambled onto one and across to another and saw Bloc Mór, it had to be Bloc Mór – large and flat and unnaturally smooth.

He admired it first.

He walked its width and stood on the edge looking into the depths. And looked out to the horizon. He had become used to the view from the cabin. The ocean was a different animal up close.

Years ago, when children would spend hours playing away from the house and beyond the awareness of their parents, he could imagine how this would be a playground, an adventure park, a television.

He was reminded of what Isaac Newton said: *I do not know what I may appear to the world, but to myself I seem to have been only like a boy playing on the sea-shore, and diverting myself in now and then finding a smoother pebble or a prettier shell than ordinary, whilst the great ocean of truth lay all undiscovered before me.*

Where did that come from? He must have read that years ago and had never thought of it since. Nothing is lost!

He sat down and let his gaze rest lightly on the place where the sky met the ocean. He became aware of his breathing. As he was breathing in he was aware that he was breathing in, as he was breathing out he was aware of breathing out. There was the sound of the water, and the birds and the feel of the wind on his face.

Then he remembered it was Christmas Day and he needed to go into the village and phone his folks. He was back on his feet before he realised he had been distracted.

He went to the four corners of Bloc Mór and came back to the middle, and looked up behind him and saw the path – the way he should have come down.

Returning up the slope, on the last bend, he took a cut

branch in each hand and trailed them behind him. Close to the cabin he leant them over the low wall with some other trunks and branches. He had wondered why they had come to be there, and now he knew.

In the shed he noticed the old bow saw with the shiny blade hanging on the nail. Now he saw the tin of lubricating oil. And the wall of cut wood, so neat that it called out to him. Everything had its place. He had wondered why and now he knew. All was being revealed. There is a method in the wilderness.

He went to the phone box in the village.

16 TO 1

THE sea was always doing its thing. Motion, in waves and white-tops. Colour, in shades and shadow. This headland, when the sun was out and the sky was blue, was picture-postcard beautiful. The rest of the time the sea heaved with a more subtle beauty.

"What happened to me? I was caught by my success, my career. I was careering alright! As my income increased my lifestyle had morphed to absorb it until my 'needs' and 'wants' were in control. I was just doing my best to keep up."

Streaky was explaining how he came to move back to the village.

"Growing up here, maybe there was an unconscious fear, extreme poverty was such a recent memory, I guess it made it easier to believe in the need to succeed financially, materially. Maybe. I found school work easy so when I went to the city there were opportunities aplenty. Quite quickly I had a handful of businesses, each one burgeoning! Each morning I cycled through the city to work because it was quicker than driving. When my bike got a puncture I took it to the repair shop rather than fix it myself. Once I couldn't be bothered to wait, I bought a new bike. Sitting at my computer, I had a window open at the bottom of my screen, watching out of the corner of my eye while my shares made a grand-a-day...As time went by I had more contacts and fewer friends. I remember walking round my living room one evening – I remember the feeling very clearly – agonising whether to book another holiday or buy an apartment. Of course, people thought *lucky bastard*, that's not real suffering. Having all that privilege and opportunity but no happiness is not the kind of problem you can easily talk about to most people. One morning, as I pedalled past, a silhouette opened the window blinds in a fourth floor apartment. After that, each day as I passed I looked up; the same shadow was drawing back the same curtains, at the same time. I wasn't riding a bike, it was a hamster wheel. Jaysus, I can feel my stomach going to steel at the thought of it. Anyway, there was a crash. Not in the economy. In me.

"I had been commuting and working and trying to eke an extra hour out of every hour. Straining some relaxation, enjoyment or meaning out of the business of each day. I was seeing people have a miserable time in Paradise. I saw the flaw. I was spooked by how they were duped. I was raging at how they were caged in. No matter how I thought about it, it wasn't funny or clever. It made me sick. And yet people who have no reason to smile, smile. Why? How?

"A switch flipped. A difficult decision made easy. The day you become unconvinced of the goal it is like being unplugged from the power source. Without the drive and adrenaline, my energy dipped and health suffered. For many years I was booming, now I was busted. And for what? For whom? Why?

"I was only just in time.

"I remember standing on the street, my arms fell to my side, I was looking at a waste bin. I slipped off my shoes and placed them next to the waste bin, put my socks and tie in the waste bin, and walked home.

"I let the world disappear off into the distance. I was setting myself adrift, that's what it felt like – leaving the mother ship in the middle of an ocean, climbing into a small row-boat and watching the world-as-I-knew-it sail away. There was fear and discomfort. And relief at being master of my own destiny. I had spent enough time voyaging with flatlanders – those who in the middle of a dark night, or in the heat of the day, will fall off the end of the earth. And it will be a surprise to them.

"I had seen behind the mask – everyone scrambling to end up on top. I had business partners, educated men and women, top of the class in economics school but with no 'feel' for what they were doing. They made mistakes but deflected the responsibility and so escaped the learning. I sold my companies to them, string-free and quickly, leaving me enough to begin again. And that would be a challenge – how to be simple and discerning with oceans of choice and the sky as the limit.

"Four hours sleep a night became fourteen. I couldn't think straight, only in resentful circles. I had muscles of crepe paper. Sometimes you only see how broken you were when you are on the mend. This village became a bit of a refuge. It was a metaphor for coming home, of the return I needed to make. Here I could be me. Whatever that meant, I didn't know. But slowly I remembered. How far I had strayed from the heart advice I had grown up with; if you can't help, at least don't harm. What you think and say and do is your responsibility; don't be lazy – meaning don't be selfish and short-sighted.

"I scooped a fair bit of sand myself. An old woman found me here on the beach. Something about the way I was lead her to believe I was dead. I was just sleeping.

"Mrs Murphy had come back to see her home place one last time – where the cabin is now – her brother was going to sell to a developer. She moved very slowly but never got tired. She sang the land into life. Nothing was missed, like we were walking through a picture she had painted many years before. I made notes; they are in a leather folio on the bookcase."

A car horn sounded long and hard in the village. Streaky turned, then looked back at Ed.

"I fell in love with the land and my childhood self and my potential. I got a whiff of clarity and purpose. Anyway, it's time for me to go." He jogged away.

Later, Ed found Streaky's notes from that day with Mrs Murphy. It was why Ed had searched for, and found, Bloc Mór. It was why he was moving more slowly.

The Murphy family rented a portion of this land since 1829. At that time there were sixteen families living on this hillside farm. After 1847 all the other families died out or emigrated.

"Sometime around 1940 I sent the names of all the fields through the school to be collated by the Commission on Folklore and Tradition. Probably still available in the National Library or some other stuffy shelving. Must be over fifty years since I was here last, unfortunately my memory is somewhat clouded having collected too much rubbish on my journey through life. The place names are a bit jumbled in my head. We grew early potatoes, rhubarb and onions in the more sheltered parts and hay in the open areas."

This was by way of an introduction, warming her way into it, defrosting her recollection, she was tracing the tumbled-down walls and overgrown ditches. They all have a name. And a story. Each field, some so small they are more garden than field. And the big stones which are seats and tables and signposts.

The second page had an annotated sketch map:

Bóthar na gleafall – only horse and carts used that road. On foot we went up past Tobar Mór (Big Well) and down Céim (step) on the other side.

Páirc na nGaotha – The Windy Field, stretches from our place to Lynch's – in my youth there were three families living in that house. In the summer the children slept under the hedges.

Páirc Úr – The Fresh (new) Field, very steep, stony in places and difficult to work. Needed tilling regularly.

Goirtín – the little field – more easily tilled, potatoes and oats.

Páircíní (little fields) – very sheltered for potatoes and vegetables.

Páirc 'ar offig' – Once belonged to the Twomeys, was flat enough to be ploughed – reclaimed and cultivated frequently – turnips and mangold for cattle.

Faill na nGamhan – The Cliff of the Calves – maybe because some calves were lost from there - too steep to graze and difficult to fence off.

Bloc Mór – (Big Block), as children we fished from there in calm weather. Our fishing line was an accessory, an excuse. When I was older I went there to feel part of the great mystery. The centre of a universe, where Mother Earth reveals some of her secrets.

Eisc – the flat strip of land adjoining steeper ground.

Páirc Liath – the Grey Field, in three sections, always meadow, had a grey, non-porous sub-soil.

Cnocán Fada – the long mound

Mary Cam – the ruin of a house once belonging to Mary with a hunchback.

Ed looked out of the window and down at the page and out of the window.

He walked with the notebook in his hand. It had become a letter from the land and the people who worked it. The scene was rich with the toil and reward and fatigue and feast and futility and freedom. Across this land there was no stone untouched.

He maybe understood why Streaky had hidden his dwelling behind and below the stone shed, on the edge of a cliff. Out of respect and to reduce his foot print. Why do the obvious: waste a precious piece of land while ignoring a ready-made natural rock foundation?

❧

One day, after Ed finally found the composure to sit still on Bloc Mór and stay there for a while, it was as if his mind fell away and his view expanded to include everything.

As if someone had let the kids out to play: the house-of-mind was quiet.

There was nowhere and nothing to hang a thought on.

It was real. True. He knew it.

It was not a spaced-out, impotent, vacant void but a vibrant, spacious equipoise.

Holy shit! All this time he had been looking to find *something*. Add *something*. But it happened when thoughts fell away, when he dropped his thinking mind.

In the next instant he started thinking *How* holy shit and *Why* holy shit and everything went back to always, the ideas and thoughts flooding back into the house. The kids were home! Brothers and sisters, followed by their friends, through all the doors and each of the windows, they were hungry and had muddy feet.

He was thinking, *sinking*, again.

He wasn't ready to give up thinking yet.

In some ways it was a relief. Surrounded, overwhelmed, by familiarity. Back to normal. But that was the whole point; he didn't want to be normal, he wanted to be free.

He had travelled around the globe. Several times. Now he had arrived at the only place in the whole world where ease and freedom could be found. His own mind.

❧

After that first time on Bloc Mór, it didn't really happen like that again. It must have been a fortunate, one-off happenstance.

The more Ed tried to return to a blissful state, the more chaotic it became. Wave after wave of thoughts and emotions. Unsettling and uncomfortable and not peaceful at all.

So he went back to the method, to flying a kite. Sitting comfortably, alert yet relaxed; back straight without any tension; Streaky's *Tickle your heart with your beard* helped with that one.

Mindful of the present action, aware of the breathing, eyes open, gaze resting on the horizon, and aware of the world around him. Then he began to experience the flavour of Bloc Mór once more.

❖

Whenever he remembered, he went back to Bloc Mór. Sometimes he actually sat on the rock, other times he stopped whatever he was doing and placed his mind there.

6

Journey to Himself…Natural Running

JOURNEY TO HIMSELF

WHILE he was at university Ed remembered sitting in the dunes at Oyster Bay, on the other side of the camp-fire was Quinn, the first mystic Ed had ever met. Maybe he was a mystic, maybe he was just a rogue. He fearlessly did whatever he wanted which for the last few years was spending the summers in Spain, rock climbing and living in caves. He never had any money, when he needed food he shoplifted from supermarkets, he chose his clothes from other people's washing lines.

Quinn was drunk and stoned (but in the morning he would be exactly the same), he recited the Robert Service poem, *The Men That Don't Fit In*. Until that night Ed was sure all poetry was crap. He memorised the first verse, it was easy, he felt like he could have written it himself, it was that close.

There's a race of men that don't fit in,
A race that can't stay still;
So they break the hearts of kith and kin,
And they roam the world at will.
They range the field and they rove the flood,
And they climb the mountain's crest;
Theirs is the curse of the gypsy blood,
And they don't know how to rest.

Hah ra! The problem was, ten years later, Ed had to accept the poem had three other verses. It was a lament not a celebration...

If they just went straight they might go far;
They are strong and brave and true;
But they're always tired of the things that are,
And they want the strange and new.
They say: "Could I find my proper groove,
What a deep mark I would make!"
So they chop and change, and each fresh move
Is only a fresh mistake.

And each forgets, as he strips and runs
With a brilliant, fitful pace,
It's the steady, quiet, plodding ones
Who win in the lifelong race.
And each forgets that his youth has fled,
Forgets that his prime is past,
Till he stands one day, with a hope that's dead,
In the glare of the truth at last.

In the glare of the truth, that's where Ed was moving to now. When the promise of youth has worn thin, like the UV coating on your favourite pair of scuffed-up sunglasses. He had a glimpse of resentment, that all he'd weathered was in vain.

The temptation was to avert his eyes, but the bright lights were what he had been searching for. The right filter is all he needed.

He was missing something fundamental, the basis, and it just seemed however much knowledge or experience he piled on top of it, it wouldn't stick – it was all like snow falling on water. Nothing to show. One experience folds into the next. He was still looking for that context, that sequence, that would have everything make sense.

For Ed, right now, happiness or well-being were not helpful words. They were the icing on the cake, and had a sickly feel to them – too much dependency and unreliability in the mix. He was looking for a feeling of wholeness, of completeness, of connection that he intuitively knew existed. It was tugging at him. Like an unrequited love. It was the original unrequited love. He wanted *whole-being*.

This constant feeling of 'something missing' meant it was never a level playing field. The dis-ease within himself clouded his judgement, and tipped and rolled him in unwanted ways. His decisions were veiled attempts to rectify and counter-act a downward slide away from where he wanted to be, which was a lasting happiness, which is the top of the hill.

He looked around at all the people taking partners or getting divorced. Taking the job or buying the ticket. Eating junk-food and playing video games. These great'n'small life-moves that on their own, actually, honestly, make not one bit of difference. Futile gestures.

Until he settled something within himself, his needs and wants would be at an angle. If he could level the playing field that top-of-the-hill feeling is everywhere, no?

Ed was doing the puzzle, one jigsaw piece at a time; a contentment that cannot be undermined must have the basis of inner peace.

❖

It was like the night that Nuttah went missing. Nuttah was Deb's cat. Deb called Ed, she was beside herself with worry, dozens of dark scenarios flooded her mind. So they went out in the rain calling his name, knocking on doors, shining torches into the all the places he could be, travelling in ever widening circles, and then starting again at the beginning.

135

At first light Deb put notes in letter boxes and posters up around the town before finally, exhausted, going home.

Her beloved pet was curled up in front of the fire!

He was that settled and warm she knew he had been there all along. She never thought to look there, it was too close, too obvious, too simple…

Ed cursed Deb. Then laughed at her, I mean c'mon!…But his view was changing.

One night Deb made a foolish error. But he had turned it into a lifestyle! What an idiot! And when he looked around he saw he was not alone.

Ed gave himself a good talking to. "Easy to waste your whole life searching; *they range the field and they rove the flood, and they climb the mountain's crest, theirs is the curse of gypsy blood, and they don't know how to rest.* That's how it is. I am scattered, always seeking *outside*, the last place I expect to find the solution is right here, right now.

"The cat is by the fire. So it is.

"We are restless looking for rest. I will only find rest by resting.

"The cat *is* by the fire. I can look elsewhere, everywhere. But there is only one cat, and it's by the fire.

"I am not sitting for sitting's sake. I sit down and watch my breath so, when I stand up, I have something to integrate in my everyday life. Because my habits are so ingrained it takes time to uncondition myself.

"It's not always easy. But it's the same with running – do not pass on the difficulties, see what they offer you, where they take you, what they make of you.

"Sitting down to meditative sessions is the only way to make it stick. Sitting each morning is like making that flask of tea. At various times in the day I can take a sip. Simple, easy. Sitting in Mr B, standing in the queue, cooking, washing dishes, on the beach. No expense needed, no membership necessary…"

Ed had been around the world a few times but he had never really, honestly, earnestly, with kindness and humour, looked inside. This was a buzz.

❖

One difficulty Ed had was sadness. Unexpected, that. The lighter he became, and the more inspired he was, the more he became aware of this deep sadness that accompanied him like a shadow. A shadow was a good analogy. When the sun shines it's natural that shadows appear.

It was all connected with having to re-write his story, the myth of himself. Some of the unhelpful habits and peculiar patterns were so familiar, had such a close association, were such a big part of his persona – it was his persona! If that goes what is left? If you remove the poles, the tent falls down, doesn't it?

We grieve when we are losing a part of ourselves. Quietness is a sign that part of you has died. The part that was always running away from silence.

❖

The fourth verse of the "Men That Don't Fit In" poem is this:

He has failed, he has failed; he has missed his chance;
He has just done things by half.
Life's been a jolly good joke on him,
And now is the time to laugh.
Ha, ha! He is one of the Legion Lost;
He was never meant to win;
He's a rolling stone, and it's bred in the bone;
He's a man who won't fit in.

And the last line of a Mary Oliver poem entitled "When Death Comes" says, *I don't want to end up simply having visited this world.* Amen

♦

Ed was now beginning each day by sitting up in bed and saying a prayer. He really didn't like that word though, so he didn't use it. Prayer was what religious types did. When he sat up on the bed each morning he made a heartfelt wish. One of the first times he did this, out of nowhere Emily J came to mind:

"You have to feel the feeling of your prayer, otherwise it's not answered…"

They had been sitting on the porch looking at the clouds and dark water beyond the reef. Emily would often sit there in the evenings humming and gently rocking. "…Ask and you *shall* receive – within reason o'course, just don't be asking for nuthin' stupid." she added.

"Receive from where?"

Emily stopped still and was silent for a few seconds before heaving herself around and looking at him squarely, smiling kindly, "From the other side of life o'course." She went back to her prayer and swaying.

Ed's heartfelt wish was a simple and worldly one: to refrain from harm as much as he was able and to do good whenever an opportunity arose. And to calm his mind. He found he could rescue himself from mindlessness when his breathing accompanied the action and the action was not separate from the whole picture.

He was changing the way he measured success. A good day, now was the number of times he came back to pure awareness of nowness. If he came back to pure awareness three times in one day, he could say it was a good day. In the first week. The next week it was six-a-day.

Sometimes, becoming aware of the present moment brought him face to face with the sadness. But he didn't try to change it. He just breathed with it while he continued with whatever it was he was doing. The sadness was not him. It was a feeling that had arisen, a feeling that will pass.

Sometimes it was the strength of the sadness clawing at his consciousness that reminded him he was distracted. He would catch himself believing his whole life had been a waste of time, or that the future was a dark amorphous monster, and he'd remember the breathing, be conscious of his posture, see in the direction his eyes were pointing, and hear, and smell...

He'd gotten stuck trying to reach twenty-one moments of pure awareness. He encouraged himself with the knowledge that, these days, when he remembered to be mindful he remained mindful for longer, but there were still great swathes of the day that his attention was elsewhere.

Despite his extraordinarily simple life he continued to "win" and "lose" and everything in between each and every day. But when he went to bed at night it was the 'moments of awareness' that were the measure of success, the difference between a so-called "good day" and a so-called "bad day".

◆

What will it be today? More "I" confirming accomplishment? Or will I allow the layers of fiction to peel away and accept, rest with, the instability of me?

This "Ed" is a label for a collection of causes and conditions impermanent by nature. No matter how many trophies and titles are lined up on the shelf "Ed" will never amount to more than a cup of ashes and dust.

Keeping the lie alive, balancing a pyramid on its point, was a thankless task

◆

The gate is narrow and easily missed. Is it even possible for a camel to fit through the eye of a needle? It sure is easy to feel stupid and want to give up. But I have tried everything else. Maybe if I can just make my camel very small, or the eye of the needle much, much bigger...

ED had been fed all this information. He needed to take stock. Put some shape and order on it all.

First could be relaxation. Streaky never missed an opportunity to tell Ed to relax. And to relax more.

"There is space in impossible places, where you never thought to look. Relaxation is. And continues to be. There is no end to relaxation, like the horizon it keeps moving away from you. Like the ground, keep coming back to it."

Since running the marathon he had become more sensitive to physical tension, and more accustomed to releasing it. He was more aware of physical responses to certain thoughts and circumstances. Feeling that tension, he could exhale it away.

When running down a hill there was always the fear of falling. Ed could feel himself put the brakes on, and holding tension.

"Where am I holding the tension? Release it on the outbreath. Where am I holding the next layer of tension? Release it on the outbreath."

Streaky had told him: "When things are difficult don't dig deeper, like you're ploughing up the streets. No. When the going gets tough, the wise start flowing!

"Relax and allow, as it says in the Tao Te Ching, *Let be! Then the mighty Way will act through you and its power will accomplish what you cannot do of your own volition.*

"Under threat we only focus on the danger. But relaxed… relaxed we see the big picture.

"Like a hot air balloon, shedding layers…So much of what goes in our mind leaves a residue in our body. So much that goes on in our body influences our mind. We become very full. We may even pop! It spills into our world and makes a mess. Learning to relax is learning to let it all go.

"When we feel good we often celebrate by speeding up. But we can just relax more. And go faster that way. The further and faster we run the more relaxed we can be. Exercise that is endured has much less benefit than exercise that is enjoyed. So enjoy!

"If we can relax for every moment of a seven-mile run relaxation has become our natural way of being. And we'll know how to relax in our life. Then we can focus on a different quality in our running, and in our life."

Next, so closely connected to relaxation, was the breathing, the quality of the breathing.

"The breath is our greatest friend. We may hyper-ventilate, hold our breath, sigh, yawn, or whatever – and it's all outside of our awareness. The first step is becoming aware. For example, agitation or excitement causes the breathing to be uneven and rapid. So start from where you are. First, observe your breathing without trying to change it in any way. Then we can calm and balance ourselves by letting our breathing become even and slow. In this way breath can be our greatest friend."

"So what…so what do you mean by balanced breathing exactly?" Ed had asked Streaky at the top of a hill.

"Breathe evenly through the nose and mouth. Breathe evenly the exhalation and inhalation. Develop a quality of lightness.

" Running, like any action, can be deeply felt and gracefully performed."

"How do we perform gracefully?"

"Let your breath accompany the action, because every uncontrolled movement agitates the mind."

He said if we were aware when our breathing changed, and returned to a more natural, even breathing, it not only changed our inner environment, but could even pacify the outer environment too. He also said that often our breath changed *in anticipation* of trouble that we are not even consciously aware of, that if we were sensitive to our breathing it could act like a radar warning us of approaching stress – and that by returning to more balanced breathing we could even avert it!

Breathing and posture and the state of our mind were intimately connected. During the Waterfront Marathon, later on, when Ed's euphoria had worn off, Streaky had seen the tiredness seep into Ed and marvelled at how he let the "tired stories" proliferate in his head and how his posture had changed and his mood swung.

Streaky told him how moods could feel strong, beyond our control even, and how our mental state or mood was communicated in body language. But he said it could work both ways. That posture and breath were powerful too, and that instead of trying to change our mood – which was difficult – we could bring awareness to our posture and to balanced breathing, and change our mood that way.

"You have to start small. Hercules could lift a fully grown horse. But he started small. He began by carrying a foal, he trained by carrying the little foal. Day by day, as the foal became a horse his strength increased. Begin by facing and transforming your little moods and emotions."

Streaky said it was the same with stress. When we were stressed muscle tension increased causing poor posture and our breathing became shallow and erratic. Poor posture and breathing are signals that we have lost it. They are also the route back to balance."

❖

So what is good posture? Streaky was inspired by the Tibetan understanding of the body, that it was a dynamic psycho-physical system, that when the body was twisted or cramped in some way the energy would become blocked, or when we slouched or slumped it encouraged dullness in the mind – and when we're upright and alert it not only promoted good blood circulation, but better energy flow.

"Like when you're watering the garden with a hose pipe and the flow stops, you have to go find the twist or the kink?"

"Yes. Okay. I guess it's just like watering the garden. When people are stressed, angry or competitive they clench their fists, they also stick their chins out. These are the give-away signs of that mindset. And they reinforce that mindset. I am not talking about boxers or football hooligans. I am talking about nice men and women in a bank queue, sitting in a meeting or behind the wheel of their car. Or running. So, tickle your heart with your beard. No really. Try it, try it now. Stand tall, but relax. Visualise the end of your imaginary beard barely touching the middle of your chest – see what happens to your posture – and bring light attention to the back of your neck, and of course the breathing – there you go! Posture is not just a topic for running or meditation, it is a state of mind. With good posture we are younger, healthier, more beautiful. Good posture gets us the job. And gets the job done."

When Ed sat more upright and imagined his beard tickling his heart he felt an opening or warmth at the back of his neck.

Some days when he did this it felt like his head was a basin full of dirty sock-water and correcting his posture in this way was like removing the plug to let all that pollution flow into the vast ocean of his heart, where it was insignificant, instantly dissipated.

Other days, correcting his posture, his body became more like a chimney allowing all the smoky emotions to just keep on rising and merge with the stratosphere.

Sometime there were no images, there was just a sense of release and space.

Tickling his heart with his beard, and awareness of the breathing, and feeling an opening, a freeing, at the back of his neck sometimes instantly de-congested his mind and sometimes instantly extinguished emotions. Sometimes it took a while, the rest of the day even.

"The spine has natural curves, how do I know what good posture is?" Ed had asked.

"It's subtle," answered Streaky, "Imagine a golden thread tied to the crown of your head. The crown of your head is a small bit back from the top of your head. While remaining very grounded, imagine this golden thread attached to the crown of your head pulling you firmly but gently skywards. Just a little. Feel your chin fall in, just a little. Of course you are aware of your breathing. And you are alert yet relaxed. That's good posture."

❖

Ed was finding that if he needed something extra, rather than looking for more effort, he should look to loose some resistance.

Streaky had quoted Antoine de Saint-Exuperay: *In anything at all, perfection is finally attained not when there is no longer anything left to add, but when there is no longer anything to take away.*

Try, try, try, try. Then he realised the only way is to stop trying, to stop telling himself and start listening.

Streaky was right, Ed knew it. He had proved to himself that a handful of good technique was worth spadefuls of effort.

On a raft trip in Nepal they had camped on a river-beach. It was evening. He was swimming upstream, it was effort-full, he was getting nowhere, which was fine, this was just for the exercise...until he remembered all the Saturdays and Tuesdays of his childhood, and sometimes Sundays, when his parents would drive him to swim classes, and the coaches walking up and down the poolside correcting their style.

Ed remembered that and stopped trying so hard and brought his awareness to technique. He eased it back a notch, and had his hands pulling under the body, adding the leg kick, eased it back some more, relaxed, more fine adjustment...After two minutes of swimming against the current he lifted his head, the camp was twenty metres downstream, he had made progress.

◈

What could be simpler than putting one foot in front of the other? And what could be more of a challenge than to do it perfectly? Effortlessly. As nature intended. Pure action.

Ed was forced to accept that, habitually, he did everything "to the max". Now he was discovering there was a depth and quality to the most ordinary things when he learned to "back off". Backing off just a small bit made a big difference. He could see what was going on around him. He could start communing. Streaky would often say it was about community, not competition.

One day, out running, Ed nearly trod on a rabbit. Gave him a helluva shock.

And the rabbit. It darted off in three different directions before deciding to dive under the gate and disappear across the meadow. Ed got excited. The rabbit did not sense Ed's approach. This must be *natural running!* Maybe Ed was becoming part of the big picture. Me, the rabbit, the world. It's all one! Todo incluido! Tutto compresso! A-mazing! It was like Streaky's favourite line in Dr George Sheehan's book: *The runner is coming to know...if he runs enough...that the universe is the smallest divisible unit.*

Not long after narrowly missing the rabbit Ed stubbed his toe on a boulder. Ouch!! He was still clumsy. Maybe that poor rabbit had myxomatosis.

Doc George and Streaky were way ahead of him.

It was late afternoon, he was four miles from home. To get back, his only option was to find the effortless place.

Ed could see how adversity, in the right dose, could be a great friend. How many times had comfort stupefied him? And besides, when there was no such thing as an easy life, what choice did we have but to learn to make a friend of adversity?

Streaky said something like, "When the going is good, you are learning nothing. So just enjoy. When the going is not so easy, you are learning a lot. The going is never good unless you have already learned a lot. So run up a hill, or against the wind, on cobbles or over obstacles. Not in competition, but in wonder."

Ed took inspiration from the dune daisies growing in the sand, burned by the salt-wind, yet smiling. And by buttercups growing in cracks in the rock.

Running on tarred roads, he discovered, was a great place to make friends with adversity. To learn to relax with adversity, run on a harsh, unforgiving surface. If a runner could have a good relationship with the tarmac it was a good sign for his life – joyful in the company of hard-hearted people and positive in the face of impervious circumstances. There was nothing more satisfying that making peace with a difficult person, or resolving a tricky situation.

You can't beat them, so meet them – on their terms – listen, hear.

Streaky liked to run on sand. And bog trails where if you are not fast and light you'd pretty soon be snorkelling. That's where he perfected the miss-step by bringing attention to the foot-lift. The heel barely touched the ground.

He was forever telling Ed to focus on *lifting the foot*.

"After you exhale you don't have to think about the inhalation right? It happens naturally. It's like that. Focus on a light touch, on lifting your foot, your heel barely touches…don't worry, your foot will find the ground again.

"Crossing a bog in full flight sometimes you can't put a foot down like you planned – you have to miss-the-step, stay airborne until your next foot comes down. Running on wet bog you perfect the missed-step. Kind of like cycling without brakes. And without the bike."

Ed's record of missed steps without a face plant in the bog was three. Streaky's was something like a hundred metres.

"You are in the sunshine, on the flat. You are a good runner, you look good, technique effortless. What happens to your posture and breathing in the middle of a hill or at the heart of a storm? Are you still a good runner?

"And on a wet downhill with legs of lead – are you still the master of your circumstances?

"You are a kind person and compassionate person on a Sunday morning, warm under the duvet. What about at the family Christmas, or meeting demands from colleagues on a Monday morning or a Friday afternoon, or in a queue going nowhere?

"This is why we train. Why we do not seek difficulties but we do not hide from them either. To develop a dynamic equipoise."

❖

One school lesson that stayed with Ed, probably because he did it so much, was boiling a kettle. He learned tremendous energy was needed to make water that was boiling at 100°C become steam. It was called a "phase change". The extra energy invested showed no increase in the temperature, it all went into the phase change, or transition, from water to steam. It was as if the water had to be cajoled and persuaded until it finally surrendered. It snapped. It order to become stable it had to make the leap and become steam.

Ed could feel wretched and be dumb and mistake-ridden, but that was no reason to pull the plug on all his efforts, it could still all be progress. It's just that the *change* had to be completed all the way through before it was noticeable.

And then for courage and perseverance he liked that quote from Thomas Merton: *Souls are like athletes, that need opponents worthy of them, if they are to be tried and extended and pushed to the full use of their powers, and rewarded according to their capacity.*

Sometimes difficult outer circumstances were required for the inner strength to manifest, to purify our being. Frustration was a signpost, not a dead end.

❖

Also during the marathon, when they were running side-by-side for more than three hours, Streaky had told Ed about the builder who fitted solar tubes in the roof of his Dublin apartment. This was after Streaky had burned out, and before he'd decided to get out of the city.

Two months after the builder was scheduled to arrive he called to say he would be coming that Wednesday. On Tuesday he called to say he would be at the apartment in thirty minutes.

The first thing he did was make a big mess by putting down dirty dust-cloths to catch all the dirt and dust he'd be making. Every time he used a drill or a saw it tripped the electrics. He came and went throughout the day and, even though the weather was unseasonably cold, he always left every door open. He used the washing up bowl from the sink to mix his plaster, and when he broke a small wall mirror he lobbed it out the window into the garden, hoping no-one would notice. Each evening he disappeared in a wild hurry, leaving used tissues on the window sill and saying he'd hoover up the mess the next morning.

"His mind was so full and his shoulders so heavy…"

Just hearing this made Ed angry at the builder. It touched all the times inside *him* when he had been unpleasantly surprised, disappointed, abused. Ed knew becoming angry did not help, but it never stopped him getting into it. He also got angry at Streaky for not being angry with the builder.

148

"Why? He'd just get angry back, and probably bodge the job too. I was beginning to value my peace of mind too much. I was starting to enjoy being in control of what I think, and how I feel. I was tired of giving that power to other people. And this was an easy example to practice with. I had some warning, to be on guard, vigilant: how for months he never came, and then arriving the day before he said he would. This was clearly going to be an opportunity, a gift. That Tuesday when he threw open the place and spread out his dirty dust sheets, I told myself this was not going to effect me. Whatever happened was going to be okay. With each subsequent 'surprise' I repeated that mantra to myself. *No reaction.* I was not patiently stacking up my grievances waiting for an opportunity to explode. It was like a mental Midas touch; each time an irritation and emotion arose, and I was able to let it pass, I was emboldened. It really was okay. Each time I dissolved a reaction in this way I felt freer, stronger, more in control. And it's like the builder was playing my game. He cranked up the pranks to test my capacity."

Streaky did confess to a moment of weakness. He called the friend who recommended the builder.

"Who, or what, have you sent me?" he demanded.

"I only ever knew one builder who tidied up after himself, and he couldn't build for shit," replied the friend. "You asked me did I know a good builder. Well, you've got one."

That was enough to put Streaky back on course.

"My friend had given me a straight answer. *Don't be a baby!* That was the week I understood that we should be grateful for opportunities to practice kindness. That real humour is *seeing a possibility, a space, where there was none.* And now the punchline, the insight, the secret that will stop you ever ever getting annoyed ever again? Do you want to know it? It is…Accept *what is! Accept what is* is not resignation or lethargy, and it's not denial or avoidance. *Accept what is* is balance, stability, flexibility, true, practical, real. It is the powerful place from which to effect positive change."

The builder finally left, and Streaky straightened out his magnificent apartment which was beautifully transformed by natural light filtered down through the new solar tubes.

Best and most of all, Streaky was left feeling he could manage his mind. He knew *accepting what is* brought a strong and robust peace to his mind.

"Accept what is, about yourself and about the world, and then you can go beyond it. In Zen Buddhism students practice flower arranging. They are obliged to use everything; if there are sticks and twigs and stones and grass, they all become part of the arrangement.

"Not just accept what is, embrace it! Everything and everyone gets to play.

"Once you understand something like that, a truism, you begin to see examples of it all around you. Adeu Rinpoche was in a Chinese prison for twenty years. He said, *Being imprisoned, you are not physically free; also your voice is not free, but your state of mind cannot be imprisoned by others, only by yourself. The prison guards had no idea what I was thinking...there was nothing the guards could do to control that.*"

Ed wrote a verse to remind himself:

> *Freedom is not being wild*
> *and doing crazy things.*
> *It is to be happy wherever I am.*
> *If I find peace and happiness within the mind itself,*
> *I will always be free.*

❧

A lot of Ed's friends were surfers, and if you asked surfers where they wanted to be, they would say "surfing". If you got more specific they would say "in the pocket" or "the curl", which is the point where the wave is breaking. That's the bit that packs the power. It's equivalent to the middle of a cricket bat or tennis racquet – if the ball hits that sweet spot you better hope your bat is angled right because it's gonna fly.

Running has a pocket when it becomes so efficient it feels effortless. Ed did not find it by habitually charging off in the same way he always did. He found it by tuning in, identifying where he was holding tension, checking he was following his own guidelines for good form. How? By stopping, standing, checking his posture and continuing very slowly. Breathing with…

If it worked barefoot it would always work. In the same way, if it worked when he was going very slowly it was a good sign. Speed up slowly, slow down often. Somewhere in there was the perfect form for that day, on that trail.

Ed was sure that meditation had a pocket too – when the posture and breathing were aligned and natural. He would find it by checking his posture against the instructions, tuning in to how it felt, making small, mindful adjustments during the breaks and then beginning to sit again.

❖

Sometimes it was during the breaks that the real meditation happened. Moments when it was obvious that wisdom is not something you *have*, but a wavelength you tune into.

❖

The mathematics of wisdom:
Clarity equals
a calm mind
over time.

7

Scandinavian Girl…Us…The Second Law
Ultimate Cross-Training

SCANDINAVIAN GIRL

"WOULD I like more tea?"

"It will not help."

"Will I have some more tea, anyway?"

That was a conversation he had in his own head. Ed was recognising how habitually sloppy he was. How his preoccupation with short-term well-being made the rest of his life untidy.

❖

In the morning he wakes, makes his heartfelt wish and swings his legs out the side of the mattress to stand up from the bed. He gingerly takes a step and another, his calves are fit to bust.

He makes a brew. A cup of tea can turn most situations around. In twenty minutes he will know if yesterday's run was a lot, or too much.

The inside of the mug is stained brown by the tea. Because that's what he puts in it. This morning he cleans it bright white.

His mind and heart are like the mug, coloured by his thoughts. Occupy your mind with love, he reminds himself.

He has taken to sitting in the big round window each morning and each evening.

❖

Mornings, Ed ate porridge. Oats and water. That's just about it, yet porridge can taste *so* different.

He was on his third brand of oats, but this one was clearly the best. Good sized flakes, not too big, and while they went soft, they never went to mush. Especially as he never cooked them. Just poured hot – not boiling – water over the oats, a pinch of salt, maybe a small corner of butter, placed a lid over the top and a tea cosy over the pan and went away for fifteen minutes. He would put a few raisins in to soak too.

Sometimes he didn't go away but tipped sunflower seeds into a hot frying pan, then two minutes later some pumpkin seeds, move them round a little until they browned. Took them off the heat. Stretched to the ceiling, touched his toes. Made the tea.

The porridge was ready. Pour porridge into bowl, sprinkle seeds, drizzle honey and ingest!

More recently he had put the bowl on a tray, placed a spoon neatly beside it. And a side plate with a piece of fruit and the steaming mug of tea. And sat in the window and made a meal of it. He was learning to respect himself, and the day that was in it.

He really enjoyed it. He was not only fuelling himself up for the day. This was his day. If he wrote a diary, eating breakfast would be an event he would note down.

Birdsong, the weather, his mood were all part of his breakfast. Letting the options for the day float across his mind. His imaginary diary page would be filled before the bowl was clean and the tea drained. But he didn't keep a diary because if he was writing something down he'd been missing something else. He didn't want to miss anything anymore.

❖

The fire had to be on for the warm water anyway, and he began to leave his towel by the stove. A warm towel after a good shower could fill another page in the diary!

❖

While rafting in Nepal they went down rivers on multi-day, self-supported wilderness trips. That meant you had to take everything you need. Everything the guide and crew-of-eight needed had to be packed in waterproof bags and barrels and strapped into the centre of the raft. Each person could only bring so little.

The longest river journey was the Sun Kosi – eight days. Ed was always dumbfounded when, on the seventh or even eighth morning, the Scandinavian girls would emerge from their tents in fresh, white, pressed T-shirts.

Ed would be cooking breakfast, wearing the same short-and-vest uniform he always did. When he heard the tent zips he'd lift his head from the fire and move the dreads out of his eyes, and see them emerge with glossy, perfectly groomed hair and a crease down the middle of their cotton trousers – visions spontaneously arising, goddesses stretching in the morning sun.

How was that possible? Clearly it was extreme behaviour and not to be encouraged! But Ed was starting to see Scandinavian tendencies creeping into his own life, a little of that care and tidiness creeping into his own behaviour. And he liked it. This way life was fussless. Being lazy, he decided, was quite effortful – like not oiling the chain on your bike. Yuk and ouch.

Next out of the tents, still in time for breakfast, were the Germans and Dutch – presentable but nothing special. The Irish sat up wherever they were, they often never made it to their tents. Other nationalities followed, having to rush their breakfast and spilling most of it down their front.

❖

It was February. Ed was standing looking at a bright green patch of vibrant young stingy nettles. He remembered how one June day in Austria Esther had lamented to the other raft guides that the nettles had lost their sting and their colour and were flowering and she was missing her morning brew of nettle tea.

What a crock of shit! Ed had drunk tea, real tea, from a bottle as a baby, and had never looked back. The idea that tea could be made from nettles and weeds was very strange. Esther was Dutch, so he let it go.

155

It was February and Ed was standing looking at the bright green patch of vibrant young stingy nettles. He picked a few of the young heads, felt the keen sting, took them inside, put them in a pot and poured hot water over them, sat down with a cup next to the pot, and waited.

He drank it in. It was a full taste. And like porridge it reached the extremities and came back to his heart. He whispered an apology to Esther from Holland. He was apologising a lot these days.

◆

The ocean moderated the climate, it was never too cold, frosts were rare. Ed was hand-washing his clothes. A natural selection had taken place – everything unnecessary had been folded away and ignored in the back cupboard of Mr B.

He was down to two of everything. Shirts and underpants, that is. Everything else he had one of. One hoodie, board-shorts, and jogging trousers (which he never wore for jogging, just around the house and trips into the village or town). And a pair of woollen socks for just around the house. He wore the brogues, sock-less, when he went for a run or into town. So his "wardrobe" was small and all he needed.

His favourite shirts, the ones he was wearing now, were from Tenzin's shop in Kathmandu. Tenzin bought them from expedition members returning from the mountains and needing to pay off debts and buy flight tickets home. They were of the best quality, warm, light and quick-drying.

Streaky's dad had said, "I'm too poor to buy cheap stuff." Ed liked that. Quality counted. With good care these shirts would last forever.

And he had a blanket. On cold days, or in the evenings, Ed wrapped himself in a blanket. He didn't wear the blanket into town; people would think he was strange. He wore the hoodie in town.

156

In some respects Ed was turning into a Scandinavian girl.

❧

He had lost weight. He was thin anyway but now he was fatless. No excess. It began in his head. Appreciating small things, taking simple pleasure. Drops of dew, the breeze on his face, the taste of food. He took the time and saw that less was more.

And less was less too.

"With our thoughts we make the world," Ed read in the *Dhammapada*. Every action had a reaction, every cause, an effect. A calm mind needed less, consumed less, discarded less.

Mindfully folding his sleeping bag in the morning calmed his mind. Returning into the room to see the sleeping bag neatly folded calmed his mind. A calm mind has fewer questions. Breathing mindfully, not being wasteful with sighs, or breath-holding and gasping his way through the day.

Like drinking a glass of water. He took half-a-mouthful, moved it around his mouth. Tasted it. Felt it. Mouth watering! After a few seconds he swallowed it slowly. That is refreshing!

❧

Nothing was more simple than slipping out the side door for a run. But without awareness, the complications could creep over him like ivy on an empty house.

Shoes, socks, bags, hats, drink, watch, heart monitor, snacks, camera, money, spare things *in-case*. Pockets bulged into bags and all too soon he would be back-packing.

In case is a cop out. *In case* is never ending. *In case* is a mind trap.

❧

There are 100 ways to run;
99 of them are not right.
The joy is to find the effortless 1.

US

FOR the first time in his life Ed was leaving some space for answers, or at least allowing some time to become clear about his confusion. He was waking up to the human condition.

He reflected how no-one has only pleasure and no pain. And no person had the praise who will not one day receive the blame. And no-one will always lose and never gain. And anonymity is all that is left after fame.

That is the nature of life. This is the perspective, how it is. It is like that. That's liberating. In that light, all jealousy and all anger and all pride are set free.

And time does not stand still. There is a time to earn and there is a time to spend. A time and also a need. Every person and place has its time. Time does not stand still. Life is alive. We are all on the same trip.

He was waking up to fellow humans – how we should humbly celebrate our own success and share our good fortune while we have it, and we should celebrate coming second – or last – give the victory of others. It's the least we can do.

That happiness is not a competition, or a finite resource. It does not come to me instead of someone else, or to me when someone else has finished with it. It is not dealt out or divided between, it is open, free and available. It comes when I am ready.

He was convinced of that for a moment, and in that moment there was boundless generosity in his heart; he wished happiness for everyone, and when he saw the success and joy of others he would only want it to last, and to grow.

It's their time, their turn. They surely deserve it, have paid for it, or will pay for it. Enjoy, enjoy!

A pile of sand can only be so tall, and so steep. Subject to the wind of change.

◆

There was a shift happening. His *gladiator pit* mentality was softening, transforming, becoming a *band of brothers* perspective; we are all facing the same hardships and uncertainty, and share a common goal. We can share the goal, we don't have to compete for it.

Before, through indifference and fear, he put everyone else on the same lowly level. Now he saw others as equally important, as worthy of happiness as himself. Even more than himself.

That was quite a leap. Competition is something he grew up with, he learned in school. He left school thinking that. His final exams proved that – only a certain percentage got the "A" grades. And however well everybody had done, a certain number had to fail. It's how the world works. Except it isn't.

❖

Two voices hold us captive.

Hope is well-dressed
driving the fast car
there is a whisper to say
that should *be me.*

Fear is on the bridge
a cup in his outstretched arm
that could *be me*

❖

Self gratification for dummies, it's like this...

Change one small thing, everything changes. Look how easily the word laughter becomes slaughter. How easily joy can become sorrow. And joy again.

With one simple twist, or untwist, something awful can be perfect. Sometimes it's just another way of seeing.

We all know that when you give, then you receive. The problem is we want to receive first.

In this context if there is any small thing you can do to brighten the day of someone else, do it. Why not? You will discover the great spiritual secret; helping others helps you.

We can be selfish and wise at the same time! How? By understanding that helping others helps *me*, harming others harms *me*.

People say that being selfless demands faith and courage; Ed was beginning to see how that could be true. But it's also so logical, Mr Spock of the *Starship Enterprise* could have ghost-written some of the Buddha's teachings. Helping others helps *me*, harming others harms *me*.

Ed looked at his life. And his family, his community, his virtual community – he went global – all he could see were examples confirming this one: helping others has helped *me*, harming others has harmed *me*. It's happening all around him. And the most content people live in the service of others.

Feeding someone rope so they can trip or hang themselves is not help. Genuine help comes from a pure motivation, wishing to relieve the suffering of others *and* bring them lasting happiness. It is answering the need of the recipient, not filling a void or satisfying the ego of the actor. And whenever Ed had faked it he had been found out.

With right intention and pure motivation any action, every action, can be a service.

If we are a collection of atoms
and they are all energy and matter.
Is it true that
the less 'I' matter
the more energy 'I' become?

❖

Ed had noticed the number of holiday homes in the village.

On the beach one day he experienced an intimate moment between a child and her father. They were preparing to go home, and Dad was shaking the sand out of her sandals.

"Dada, why do we need two houses?"

The purity and innocence in that voice, the common sense and wisdom of the question hung in the air for a few golden moments.

"So we have somewhere to go on holidays sweetie, c'mon, up we go…"

A tea-spoon of bullshit was all it took. No need for a land-slide of adult reasoning or pages of small-print. The child may ask the question again later in life, she may not.

Ed was sure we will always live in a world where some people have three homes and others are homeless. Doesn't mean we ever give up trying to address the balance. We may not be able to give them a home, they may not want one, but we can help them feel more at home with their situation.

Some day we may realise a person does not need to live next door to be our neighbour.

❖

Around then is when Streaky told Ed about rich-people suffering. Ed had never considered this. Rich people had what he wanted, why would he have compassion for them? If they had a bit of *his* misery they would know what it was like, but only until they bought themselves out of it.

Streaky gave him the example of an affluent couple sitting on a tropical beach who order champagne. When it arrives it's not cold enough. That really is a bummer! To get there that couple got really lucky, or worked really hard and made a lot of sacrifices, or accumulated a lot of negative karma organising a successful scam. Whatever. They paid big bucks for the champagne and now it's warm and the waiter has disappeared…

"Money makes it easier, sure," continued Streaky, "but it does not make you immune. You have more opportunity, more expectations and fewer excuses. The more possessions you have the more you have to insure, repair, guard, lose. Wealth can be just as big a challenge to peace of mind as poverty. Only your mind can put you permanently and irrecoverably beyond suffering. So long as we look outside of ourselves for happiness, we will *never* be free from frustration."

He said in developed countries our suffering is often mental suffering. It only happens in our head.

"As the Dalai Lama once observed, you can live in the best apartment in New York, with a view out over Central Park, but if your mind is messed up all you are looking for is a window to jump out of! And that stuff happens. Look at all the Hollywood suicides.

"Rich people do not get what they want either. Once they have got it, they don't want it any more. That's why they are not really happy. Nobody gets what they want. It's how the world is. Happy people have learned to want what they get. And they don't want much. Which is what they get. And they are happy with that. Their happiness effects the people around them, who in turn support their state of mind. That's what it is – a state of mind.

"We need to be simple. We need to be how *it* is.

"The *nouveau riche* of the future will be those who have very little yet are content, who lead simple lives but can count their blessings. Their new wealth will be mastery of their own mind and the spirit of community."

THE SECOND LAW

IT was raining hard. Had been for days. Ed was in the library hogging the computer again. The week before he had read

162

about the Second Law of Thermodynamics and then later the same day he saw heart-busting news pictures of a boat that had sunk – a boat that was just twenty metres long and had been carrying 500 Africans on a voyage of just 113 kilometres to a new life in Europe. The boat sank a few hundred metres off of the Italian island of Lampedusa, the closest European landfall.

Ed decided the two were related. The world was in a mess, and people talked about a *melting-pot*; somehow the Second Law of Thermodynamics would give him the answer.

The Second Law said that over time differences (in temperature, pressure, and density) tended to even out.

Taking heat as the example, the second law predicted that the flow of heat would be from a region of high temperature to a region of low temperature. When this process occurred, the hot region became cooler and the cold region became warmer. The transfer happened in that direction only, from hotter to colder, never the reverse. The temperature differences thus tended to diminish over time.

Even before it was announced, Ed knew that Europe's reaction to the African migration would be better border controls and refugee camps. And so on.

But according to the Second Law this migration would be a relentless, natural flow until we look into Africa and take the heat out of that situation. Until Africa was a little more like Europe. Until we look fearlessly into the heart of the problem instead of applying band-aid solutions. We can roll our eyes at the impossibility of it all or look fearlessly into the heart of the situation.

Ed read more on the Second Law, and his heart was sinking. The Second Law showed that differences in heat (or pressure or chemical potential) decrease over time, leading eventually to "heat death" – when the universe would have no thermodynamic free energy to sustain motion or life.

Yikes! Was he understanding this right? Not only did differences diminish, so did the energy, and the process was not reversible.

Then a glimmer of hope called the *oscillating universe theory*: the universe would end in a collapse or "big crunch" followed by another big bang, and so on.

Okay. Why didn't that make him feel any better?

Ed did some thinking; perhaps by then humankind would be able to "jump ship" to a parallel universe that was further away from its ultimate decline than this one…was that helping? That was not helping.

Okay. Try this.

The Second Law confirmed our human experience: we lived in a one-way universe where time went forward. Glass could break but it couldn't unbreak. You could turn a piece of wood into ashes, but no one had managed to reverse that process. We grow older, never younger.

But, he read, the Second Law was the scientific black sheep. Every other fundamental law in physics, including the laws that describe the dynamics of atomic and subatomic particles, described a two-way universe. A universe *without* an "arrow of time". So the arrow of time might only be true in a world observed at macroscopic level – for the world of aggregates, such as human beings – rather than the particles or atoms.

He took a breath. He thought he might have understood that. From a human perspective it was bad news. Charles Eugene Guye said, "It is the scale of observation that creates the phenomenon." To calm down he should think atomic, or smaller.

Once calm, he read through his notes again and found another piece of hope: the Second Law of Thermodynamics was only true for isolated, closed systems where there were no external influences. For example, why the cheese melted on his burger.

Ed went outside, paced through the square, leaned against the beech tree, looked up into the branches, paced again. The answer would not be found in the world of aggregates or in a closed system. The answer would need to be invisible, unmeasurable and immeasurable.

Yes! He had it! The force that could change the world, address the balance, halt the decline, raise our consciousness, was Love. Its manifestation was compassion. Love and compassion would save the world. If we let it. Right?

We live in a world where sodium, which is a metal, can be combined with chlorine, which is a toxic gas, to become table salt, which is edible and harmless…Of course it was possible!

◆

Theories can be dangerous, Ed knew that. They were a fixed position, a determined point. Once he had a theory it was usually easy to gather the evidence to substantiate it, to convince himself he was right.

As a child he can remember saying that he hadn't seen a red car all day. After that there were so many red cars.

Now, he was a bit older, it was like that with love and compassion. It was out there. He just needed to look for it with childlike openness.

◆

Streaky told him that the Buddhists say that this body – this life – is like a boat, a boat that can carry him to the shore of salvation or sink him. In that case he was a migrant, an asylum seeker, fleeing the suffering and frustrations of a difficult life, hoping for a better future.

So where was he heading? What was his Lampedusa? Or was he drifting in a vast ocean, moving in an unknown direction until he capsized or ran out of steam?

ULTIMATE CROSS-TRAINING

ED was running a lot, running further and faster. And was discovering a new quality of awareness. Thinking less and smiling more. But he was also stubborn.

Streaky said, "What you still don't grasp is that meditation is not some hippy dippy optional extra. It's the essential warm-up, the ultimate cross-training for running, and for life, and even for death. "

◆

"How are you doing?" asked Ed

"Good – really good!" replied Streaky

"What's happening?"

"Actually, nothing – really nothing!"

Unlike Ed and his wild stories, Streaky was very ordinary, living proof that happiness, the stable, reliable kind, was boring. It was when things were quiet and no thing, and no thinking, was happening.

"Use the stories of your past to spur you on, transform regret into a resolve to change, to live a meaningful life.

"I love running but meditation has given me as much, more even. Meditation has made me more like the person I want to be."

The biggest part of Ed was still much more interested in how far he could run and how good it felt, than what direction he was going in. He was beginning to understand that the same challenges existed in his meditation as in his running, as in his life. That meditation could be the ultimate cross-training. That he could learn a lot by sitting down and setting his mind free. Ed already knew that running a very long way was easy compared to sitting quietly, undistracted, for even a short time.

He could sit, his body still, for a short time, apparently peaceful, but his mind had been around the world a few times. He could be in his favourite place, but if his mind was elsewhere where was *he* really?

Neither here nor there.

❖

Learning to leave his mind in meditation could be compared to snorkelling, which is breathing with one's face under water. Which is just wrong!

It had taken a lot of time and nagging for his brain to get used to snorkelling, for all those doubts and questions to be overcome. For him to relax and just breathe.

Learning to leave the mind in meditation was such a challenge, when there was a gap in his thoughts, when a space opened up, to resist the temptation to immediately fill it up, to relax and just breathe.

❖

Another bookmark: *There is no contentment in distraction, all doing should be done from a state of* being. – Sogyal Rinpoche

8

Mad…Impermanence of I…Incarnation

MAD

ED entered the library but was ushered straight out again by Deirdre the Librarian. Reading was a popular pastime in the town, especially among the menfolk. They attended poetry readings and signed up for computer courses. They wore ironed shirts to surf the internet, or check the community noticeboard, or loudly offer their erudite opinion around the coffee machine. There were reading circles and writing groups. And Deirdre was at the centre of the mandala.

Deirdre span elegantly on her toes – she had painted nails – and locked the library door and turned again, slipping the keys into her bag, and her bag over her shoulder.

Deirdre was poetry in motion. Ed could feel a composition coming on. Her sunglasses were up on her forehead holding back long tresses of raven black hair. She wriggled her brow and the glasses dropped onto her nose and some of that hair fell around her face.

"I assumed you'd be here today," she said. "You were nearly late."

Ed looked at the closed and locked Library door. His mouth opened, no words came out.

"Hurry or we *will* be late. This way," she instructed stepping off the pavement.

Ed followed Deirdre down the main street; all that was missing was a leash. He wondered if this would count as a date.

Hope did a little skip in his heart. She turned left and started up the church steps.

Deirdre crossed herself and indicated to Ed which pew to sit in and slid in next to him. Keep calm, he told himself. They were early for whatever it was they were attending. As the congregation arrived Deirdre leaned in a small bit and asked him if he had ever heard of Mad King Sweeney.

He so wished he had. But he hadn't. And he was very busy trying to contextualize the last three-and-a-half minutes. All this was communicated in the blank look on his face.

"Before the Battle of Moira in AD 637," Deirdre started, "King Sweeney was transformed into a bird by Bishop Ronan's curse. The Bishop had mocked Sweeney, or so he thought, so Sweeney, who angered easily, launched a spear at the Bishop, missed him but impaled one of his assistants, so the Bishop cursed him anyway. Sweeney's curse was a sensitivity to noise so it took dramatic effect when the King led his army into battle at Moira; amongst the clamour and cries this once proud warrior was gripped by a mental torment, he dropped his weapons and his armour, his nobility and pride, and all the other stuff that keeps us bound to this earth and, with nothing holding him down anymore, he escaped on the wind.

"They say he was transformed into a bird but the translation I prefer says he became *a creature of the air*. He became a creature of the air, not a bird, it's not the same at all at all at all. He was 'away with the birds', his mind was light and free, but he was not a bird.

"He ran with a feather-like touch, hardly disturbing the dew. He took the path less trodden, because contact confused him. He remained alone, because no-one could catch him. Living in trees. Looking out from above.

"In the darkest parts of the night, and in the cold light of an infant sun – his feet bitten by the frost and the wind nipping at his frame – he knew he was alive. He saw the sorrow and sadness. And freedom and ease, and how it was so achingly close yet we don't see it. Like our own face.

"He saw a sunny day was just a day without clouds. He was alive. And could not sleep. How could he? He took the pledge that as long as unruly men suffer from manic desperation he would manifest as their protector. Because unruly men, more than any, need a guide don't you think? They are unruly for a reason. Relieved of that reason they can be reasonable too, no?"

There was some fussing going on at the front of the church.

Deirdre's eyes went very big. "Sometimes it's so easy to believe this physical world is just a gateway to the other, don't you think?"

"Yes," said Ed, because he wanted to agree with her.. "And... What happens next?"

"That's a good question," she said "It depends what you mean by *next*. The next lifetime, or the next year or next month, or next week? The future can be the next moment, which is indistinguishable from this one, which is now. So there is no next, only this moment, *now*."

Ed's mind began to expand but as soon as it reached the walls of his skull he panicked. "I mean to King Sweeney, what happens next to King Sweeney?"

"Well, Sweeney was behaving outside the norms of men and given the label *mad*. Actually he was just arriving at his senses."

"Oh, you don't judge a book by it's cover," Ed said. Deirdre was used to inane comments from single men. Her look wiped the smile from his face. She continued,

"There are two kinds of madness: the common kind when someone is overcome by demonic powers of the psyche, and the even more common kind which is believing in the conventions and concreteness of the mundane world. Somewhere in the middle there is sanity. One thing we can be sure of, it's fierce thin up here" – she put a finger on her temple.

Ed would not be able to survive another vaporising look; a comment was required and it had to be a good one. He was blank and scared. Then one of Streaky's bookmarks flashed up in his mind. Here goes.

"The naked man who cuts himself with a knife and runs through the snow, and jumps in the frozen lake, even he just wants to be happy."

Deirdre looked at Ed and then at her hands and then at Ed. "Yes," she said. "Indeed." And a tear fell down her cheek.

The church was full now. The priest was up the front and there was more activity…and some announcements…This was the anniversary mass for Patrick Sullivan of East Gate in The Town, and John "Streaky" Cameron, of the Village Parish.

"Wha…did he say?…What? Anniversary mass, like for someone who is not living anymore? As in dead? A year ago?"

"That's right." Deirdre put a hand on Ed's shoulder. "How long did you know him?"

"Uh, not long, I think not long…"

She talked on, loud enough for Ed to hear but not disturbing their neighbours. "Our lives together have been so complicated, next to impossible. We both took the pledge you see, not to rest until all human beings have seen their innate fundamental goodness and the world is abiding in peace. Well, there is an army of us, and we all made the same promise, and we are all working together. And it's what all humans want – liberation from suffering and lasting happiness – that's what we are selling! I mean, how difficult can it be? We thought we'd wrap it up in one generation. Well ha ha! We were wrong.

"We take ordinary births so as never to lose our connection and so our lives can be an example. Some times it works spectacularly well, which makes the failures a little easier to bear. Often it's heart-breaking. There are always lots of people being very kind to each other, and lots of other people being very cruel to each other, and everyone else locked in the middle getting by the best they can.

"I think this time the images that will stay with me are of polar bears floating away on tiny islands of ice, and the flies in the eyes and bloated bellies of starving children, and still all the ambivalence. Why do people wait until it's too late before they do something as simple as change their mind? Even when they ask for help they keep such a distance, and are so easily distracted.

"The myths say that The Seers had magical powers, that we gave ancient kings the power to rule. But it was not just kings, it was anyone. Sometimes we are attractive, but more often we manifest as a difficult person or ugly situation in order to reveal the beauty in others, to open their eyes and their heart. We help the brave, whoever they are, to overcome and master their selfish hopes and fears so that they might seize control of their mind and their life. That is what is meant by giving beings *the power to rule*. That's regal. And we all have that potential."

She reached into her handbag and pulled out a folded piece of yellow card. "A book was returned to the Library after…later, this note was left in it – maybe I'll give it to you."

In the church people were singing a hymn. But Ed had entered his very own dream sequence. The real world seemed a long way away. He was aware of the voices around him but they were distant. He stood up when everyone else stood up. Shuffled down the pew and joined the human traffic moving down the aisle in the direction of the stained glass windows in the giant church doors. He looked over his shoulder half expecting Streaky to be there. Of course he wasn't there. He never was there. Fierce thin indeed.

The sun was out. It was very bright. The whole world was over-exposed.

"The library is open again Monday," Deirdre said to Ed but looking elsewhere, and she disappeared around the corner.

Ed looked at the book he still had in his hand. The library is open again Monday. The book will be overdue by Monday.

He went to The Copper Kettle, ordered a coffee and a glass of water. He drank the water and left.

◆

Heavy rain had blown the stream out of all proportion. And the wind was confusing everything. A frenzy of not-knowing. No tides today. The sea didn't look like the sea at all. It was the world's washing up bowl, the morning after. Cold. Brown. The world was in Sunday mourning.

Then a wind moved the heavy curtain of grey cloud and the sun peeked in, lighting up the patchwork fields on the mountain.

◆

Ed felt very fragile. Like if someone touched him he'd crumble. "How much of everything is in my head?"

Ironic this. Just as his mind was beginning to quieten and he felt clearer, everything was getting blurry. He wasn't sure if he was entering a new world, or just collapsing the old one. Maybe both.

Streaky was dead. Always was as far as Ed was concerned.

"How about if, just for a moment, I stop trying to understand. How about if, just for a moment, I just stay present."

The only thing that was of any help, that kept him grounded, was flying his meditation kite. It was all very simple and childlike. Just like if you counted the pennies the pounds would count themselves, he was reduced to *if you take care of the present, the future takes care of itself.*

It was working. It had to.

No wonder the locals had crossed over the road or ducked into their houses when they saw him trotting towards them in his home-made shoes, chatting and laughing to himself.

But when Ed rewound the story, slowly, a small bit at a time, he was relieved to find it was all harmless. The ghost of Streaky had not led him to a cliff-edge and encouraged him to fly, or proposed ritual sacrifice of children and animals. There were no snipers outside or police helicopters overhead. Ed laughed, remembering a story from the archives, how Harris evaded three quarters of the South Wales Constabulary including their aerial support unit.

◆

Out of his bedroom window Harris's friend Old Man Prosser could see the searchlight scanning his field. His farm was like a war zone. Flares and searchlights and mega-phones and racing engines and helicopter noise. Prosser always slept fully dressed sitting in his favourite chair – he never knew when the herd may need him – but his cap had fallen down somewhere behind the chair and Prosser never went outside without his cap on. By the time his cap was found and on his head and he was across the yard and over the road all the drama had moved down the coast. Silence and darkness.

"Pross?…is that ewe?"

It was Harris walking out of the night. He was covered in muck…

Harris had never mentioned it since but, even fourteen years later, if Prosser has had a few pints, he would still tell the story about the night that Harris hid under his cow.

"Ee was clinging to the leg of my cow, ewe see. That way the in-for-red 'eat cameras in the 'elicopter couldn't detect 'im… 'ell of a boy that 'arris…pity ee never got 'is Welsh cap."

◆

On Monday there was a man behind the desk in the library. Ed and all the other men were awkward in their surprise.

Ed handed in the over-due book and paid the fine. There

175

was a murmur in the room. Books were often brought back late, but no-one had ever had to pay the fine before.

The man who was standing where Deirdre belonged handed him a book. "You reserved this, it just came in."

Someone got up from the computer, walked quickly across the square and into McCarthy's Bar.

Ed felt sick again. He was vulnerable. Everything had to be simple. And it wasn't. Hence the sickness. He was sitting on a bench in the square. He put his hand over his chest pocket where the bookmark was, the one that Deirdre had passed on to him after the church service. He read it again. It was the same verse that had been read at his grandmother's funeral, the one attributed to Bishop Brent.

I am standing upon that foreshore, a ship at my side spreads her white sails to the morning breeze and starts for the blue ocean.

She is an object of beauty and strength and I stand and watch her until at length she hangs like a speck of white cloud just where the sea and sky come down to mingle with each other.

Then someone at my side says, "There! She's gone!"

Gone where? Gone from my sight, that's all. She is just as large in mast and spar and hull as ever she was when she left my side; just as able to bear her load of living freight to the place of her destination. Her diminished size is in me, not in her.

And just at that moment when someone at my side says, "There! She's gone!" there are other eyes watching her coming and other voices ready to take up the glad shout, "Here she comes!"

Ed looked up. Across the road, at the other side of the carpark, he could see the harbour and the trawlers moored there. He imagined Streaky's family sailing into this harbour many regatta-days before.

Streaky always said, *Refrain from harm.* Well, he had embodied that one. No harm done. And he said, *Do good.* Knowing him had brought nothing but benefit to Ed. And *calm your mind* – relax in your true nature. Maybe not right this minute, but Ed had certainly learned something about how to relax and be more natural.

He looked back at the paper. Outside the quotation marks there were a few more lines, Streaky's own commentary perhaps: *You want adventure and excitement? Then journey to the place where you can say with full understanding and confidence "dying is just another day". Dedicate this life to revealing the truth of who you really are.*

IMPERMANENCE OF I

REFRAINING from harm was not always easy. Doing good was often difficult. Relaxing while people succeeded and failed all around you was nigh on impossible.

It helped when Ed remembered death.

That's what we share. That softens the edges and the core. When kindness and compassion are difficult, remember we all have to die.

❧

Ed remembered the chapter in *Anatomy and Physiology* about involuntary muscles. There are muscles that work of their own accord, subconsciously, naturally. Like the heart, and the walls of the blood and lymphatic vessels as well as in the respiratory, digestive, and genitourinary systems. They work automatically whether we ask them to or not, they can stop working without permission too.

❧

The problem with friends is *they like you the way you are* – why would you hang out together otherwise?

And all the time Ed had wanted to change. That's why Streaky, and even Harris, and a handful of others, had been so helpful. They shined a light on his blind spots.

Streaky had told him, "You are a wave, a temporary phenomenon created by specific causes and conditions. You arise out of a deep, vast ocean, you return to that ocean, at no time are you separate from that ocean."

"Really? A wave is kinda always changing, coming and going. A frozen wave maybe?"

"In your case a frozen wave, but you do the freezing yourself. In the fruit bowl, as we speak, the pear is ripening."

◆

"If I live as if I will never die, I will die having never really lived." He was thinking about his own death, and it was helping him to appreciate life.

One day he will breathe out, and he will not breathe in again. He is dead. This is not an abstract notion. This is not a metaphor. This is how it will be. Tomorrow or the next life, which will come first? He can't say.

Gold is precious because it is limited in supply. Through reflecting on impermanence his life becomes precious. His life truly begins. In this knowledge his old life passes away, is shed like an old skin.

Ed had risked his life to feel alive. What else was there? His craziness was not bravery but desperation. He would have swapped his life for a reason to live. Some of his friends had. Drugs, drowning, falling, faking, avalanches, plane crashes. It would be a stretch to call them all friends, but they had partied together. They were all seeking the same thing.

Ed had escaped for no other reason than it wasn't his time.

Now this human birth was feeling more like an opportunity than a poker chip. He was inclined to wake up each morning feeling the days were grains of sand falling through his fingers. Not in a morbid way but like each dawn was a gift, to be un-wrapped with the eyes of a child.

For whitewater river guides it was all about speed and angle. Get it right, it was a clean run, looks easy. Get it wrong, you were swimming. Ed wanted to begin everyday with clarity and incisiveness.

❖

Ed saw how he kept setting and extending his goals to keep them valid. He starts walking, then jogging, then running. He set the goal of running to the lighthouse, The Village, The Town, the half-marathon, a full marathon, because if he kept pushing it out, extending the goal, he would never *get there* and he would never have to say "Tis done. And I am left with nothing".

He maintained the illusion, kept it alive, so he would never have to face the fact that the basket in which he was putting all his eggs of hope, meaning and fulfilment has no bottom.

❖

In college Ed had helped out a friend who put up exhibition stands. Once it was for an Over-Fifties' show. As the show began Ed walked round the giant hall. There were lots of hotels, spas, resorts and cruises. That was for pleasure – if you can afford it. Alarms, detectors, insulation and financial institutions. That was for freedom from fear – if you can afford it. And then the whole old-age-and-infirm deal: hand and face make-overs and vitamins and supplements and revolutionary cures. And you can get all your bits tested. And guess what? Your eyes, ears, back and feet are not perfect. And guess again. The very correction you need is available right there, right now!

Ed watched the people selling orthotics. They had a long queue of grey-haired folk standing in their socks. The person at the front of the line would stand on what looked like a weigh-ing scales, except it was an "ink-plate" with a piece of paper inserted in it. When the client stepped off again, an assistant retrieved the paper with a magician's flourish, and there, in black and white, was the imprint of the client's feet, which could be matched to one of the examples on the giant foot-shape chart displayed across the back of the stand.

Some of the prints looked more like a splat of ice-cream on the pavement than a foot. The sales team would then sympathetically point at the "needs help" end of the chart.

But then along comes a man whose footprint was a delightful shape. Five pinkies, forefoot, arch and heel which matched the perfect human specimen on the far right of the wall-chart. Congratulations!

Not so fast. The assistant began to predict that in ten years, or probably less, the client would experience issues . . . and prevention was better than cure.

Ed told this story to an acquaintance who happened to be an insurance broker; he described the cornucopia of stuff that people *might* need to prevent things that *could* happen.

"Oh yes, it's a good business to be in," said the insurance man, completely missing Ed's point.

Ed decided that if he wanted to live for a long time, it would be worth thinking about what kind of older person he wanted to be. And start practising that now.

Because as our life slows down our habits overtake us.

INCARNATION

ED thought about two of his early mentors who had died recently. Even after suffering serious heart attacks these men still seemed to believe that if they ignored death they would escape it, if they just kept moving they would always be one step ahead.

One of them went on wild adventures; he died on a summit

in Europe. Because of who he was, a helicopter arrived on the scene with space-age equipment and the most highly trained wilderness response team in the world. Death still won.

Another one trailed his wife behind him on holidays and outings while eating and drinking all he liked and getting red in the face with all who questioned him. The wife was a bag of nerves but she took tablets for that. He keeled over in an expensive restaurant, in the middle of a really good argument and just before the main course was served.

It was not good enough.

Thinking back, it was easier to see how and when Ed had begun to feel that there was more to life than just *this* life. Thinking back, it began in Nepal with Jim and his Cleveland Indians baseball cap.

❖

The local kids ran down the bank, chattering and giggling. Most unusual. They mostly only paid attention to the rafts as they approached white-water sections. They wanted to see people falling out and swimming or hopefully the whole raft capsized and the occupants and all their possessions dumped into the river.

This was early-season high-water river-rafting in Nepal – it does not get much better than this. And today had been "Jungle Corridor" which was always the guides' favourite. They all loved it, but Jim loved it the most.

Jim wasn't there this day because he had died in a plane crash the previous month.

For the crews of intrepid back-packers it was thrill-seeking as usual, but for the guide team it was thrill-seeking with a difference. They did not feel grief; they felt a responsibility to enjoy themselves more. To grieve you have to lose something of value. They had lost a friend, he had lost his life, but shit can and does happen. Right? It could easily have been one of them. Ed was planning to come out on that flight but his employers screwed

181

up the booking so he had to go a week earlier. He was not sure what he thought about that now, so he didn't think about it.

Maybe a week or two after the crash, Jim's dad came over from California for next-of-kin business and to see where his son had died. He came out to the house to meet the guides and look through Jim's stuff. The guides were respectful, but true empathy was beyond them. They were not parents. To think and feel deeply about anything was too much to ask. Was it lack of will, or capacity? Ed had no understanding or appreciation of life; it was often difficult and messy – maybe the end of life just simplified things.

Jim's dad took a few items that meant something to him and left everything else in a box which he asked them to use or lose. The Cleveland Indians baseball cap was in there.

The previous season Ed had offered good money for that hat, and then his Russian spy camera in a swap, but Jim would not let it go. Now it was Ed's, just like that!

So they are on the river, without Jim, it's high-water, it's morning, the sky is clear, the sun is out, and downstream the whitewater is leaping and sparkling, roaring and churning.

It's a great day to be paid to be guiding a raft down "Jungle Corridor", a wild section of river, confined in a spectacular gorge. It was an even better day to be in a kayak, watching for any swimmers, ready to ferry them back to their raft. Ed was in a kayak.

Usually when running a river the guides would pull in upstream of a whitewater section so they could inspect it from the bank, searching for any fallen trees that might be a hazard, or fallen rocks that had created obstacles or changed the channel since their last trip.

They would stand on a vantage point, gesticulating with bronzed arms, calling over the roar of the water. They wore the obligatory designer sunglasses held in place, from morning 'till evening by the equally obligatory retainer band.

But this was the early season high; the river was pulsating with brown monsoon rain mixing with ice melt. It was big and fast. There were few places for them to pull over and inspect what was downstream. With hardly any pause to collect themselves, the river had to be run "blind". This was the early season high-water rafting, and Jungle Corridor did not disappoint.

After an exhilarating morning the expedition stopped at a beach for lunch, reliving the morning and looking forward to a relatively lazy float to the evening camp.

With lunch packed away, Ed gave his helmet and life-jacket to the rafts and let them set off while he took a few minutes to doze in the sun.

He was suddenly woken by the sound of thunder. It took a few moments to remember who and where he was before slapping on his cap and shades, jumping in the kayak and pushing off downstream.

But the sky was not the only place where there had been an unexpected and unwanted change. He was not much farther down the river before he had to pull over for a toilet stop.

There he was, wedged between a rock and hard place, with his shorts round his ankles, and the world falling out of him when directly above the heavens split in two with an almighty crack of lightening and thunder, sending a chill through his body.

Back on the river, desiccated and alone.

The river was not gleaming in the sun anymore, it was dark and strange. So the chattering children running down the bank were a welcome sign of life and warmth for a moment, until he got to thinking that the children only came to the river at a place and a time of high drama.

The children stopped at the bend and opened their mouths. As he passed them he started spinning in the whirlpool, the back of the kayak drawn around and down, going vertical, spinning, before it disappeared under the surface, where it spun some more.

Some time later it bobbed back to the surface. Ed righted it at the second attempt, coughing through his nose and eyes as well as his mouth. His shades were round his neck, he was nearly garotted by the retainer band. The Cleveland Indians baseball cap was gone.

Even through the filter of water-clogged ears he heard the children celebrate. And a more distant roll of thunder.

He lifted his eyes to the heavens and looked inside of himself, "What the hell?"

A duck flaps its wings after a shock to release the tension in it's body. Ed flapped downstream. The irony was too strong to escape even him.

The cap was not his. Jim had reached out from the grave, on this day, in this way. There was no space for ambiguity.

Ed was smiling. He was not sure why.

Maybe *the why* was not because he was alive, but that he had a little bit cheated death, again. Maybe *the why* was because he had "a story" and his life to date had been about collecting stories, and joining them together and saying "this is me".

Probably *the why* was awe. He had not asked for it, he did not necessarily want it and he would not risk it on anyone else's sensibilities, but now he had all the proof he himself would ever need that death was not the end.

He also had the strong sense that wanting something was not helpful. Wanting was not helpful before, during, or after the object.

At camp, talking to the other guides, he told them about the whirlpool. On the big bend…before the Bhote Kosi tributary…

Nope. They'd seen no whirlpool.

◆

184

Ed saw the sun on the ocean and felt the wind on his back. Four seasons in a day is what they say.

The ocean becomes air-borne, floating as a dark cloud, falling as rain into the bed of the stream, rushing loud and lean. Dramatic drops and swirling pools, then broader, slower, clearer.

Meandering back to mother to begin again another life.

9

WOOD

ED picked up the bow saw, held it up and looked at it – like a falconer admiring his bird.

This was a chainsaw-free zone. Cutting wood by hand is where it's at. Relaxing, enjoyable, satisfying. A job that had a beginning and an end. It keeps you warm at the time and in the future. It has atmosphere.

In the early days Ed had wondered why Streaky didn't just have an oil tank and be done with all the effort and mess. Maybe he'd blown his fortune?

But it had become clear to Ed that "poor" was watching soap operas or bad films. The fact he had the time to cut wood meant he had all the wealth in the world.

He breathed in and breathed out while he cut the sally willow and rhododendron branches that grew like a weed. He limbed the branches and leant them against a wall or another tree according to size.

He brought the seasoned branches up to the trestle fashioned from a wooden pallet and cut them into lengths that measured exactly from his wrist to his elbow. He stacked these logs against the wall in the shed. He was not cutting the wood; as he moved the saw over the branch, the blade was cutting the wood.

The smaller pieces, even twigs, went in a basket as kindling. Nothing was wasted.

There were no flower beds, the garden was wild without

limits. Yet the wood, harvested into stacks and piles, spoke of love and care and beauty and nature.

After each use he put a drop of oil on the blade of the bow saw, using his finger to run it along the length of the blade. He did it after each and every use, so even through the dampest winter it would stay sharp and never collect rust.

He filled a wood basket one log at a time, and a second basket for sticks, and placed them either side of the stove.

He cleaned the glass window in the stove door with newspaper scrunched into balls, wetted and dipped in the cold ash of last night's fire. He rubbed the ashen paper over the inside of the window. The soot comes clean off – effortless when you knew how.

He emptied the tray of ash onto the field, or in the compost.

He set the fire in a certain way; although the stove was small there was enough room to stand three smaller logs vertically on left, and three more on the right, with the paper and twigs and sticks in the centre. With a match it all came to life and he closed the door with the draught fully open, and through the clean window the little fire licked and swallowed the sticks and, if the dry logs standing on the left and right didn't tip into the flames of their own accord, he opened the door and helped them with the fire iron.

Streaky had not written a manual. These were Ed's observations; he had cut and oiled and sorted and stacked and cleaned and set according to the system he had found in place. It had become his mindfulness practice. Whenever he was doing it differently or distractedly, he'd catch himself and begin again.

Every uncontrolled movement agitates the mind.

All doing should be done from a state of being.

Come back to the breath. He continued to win and lose and everything in between but "moments of awareness" had become his measure of success.

He let his breath accompany every action.

American Indians knelt to pray for the life of the animal they had just taken, with a pledge not to waste the meat, or the bones or the skin.

When he put the logs on the fire, he included everything a piece of tree represented: the sun and the moon and the wind and the waves, thunder and lightning, and the rain and the soil and the bugs . . .

For a long time Ed had ricocheted between intensely neurotic over-caring or complete "fuck-it" mode.

Now he had some middle ground, he was appreciating simple pleasures.

If he couldn't appreciate simple pleasures how would he ever enjoy a busy life full of more complicated pleasures?

HARRIS ON TOUR

THERE was a knock at the door. There had never been a knock at the door before.

Harris was standing on the flagstone step brandishing his bright red passport like a badge.

"It's me, Scrambles, I've come to Ireland!"

He wanted to surprise Ed and he was not disappointed,

"Ewe look like ewe've seen a ghost."

"Well actually... Jaysus, Harris... You don't need a passport to come to Ireland."

"Ewe abso-bloody-lutely do. Even if the customs boys don't ask for a look. Respect demands it. Talking of respect, the lady in the Post Office told me ewer squatting! Took me bloody ages to get 'ere, everybody looks at ewe, not like ewer a stranger but like ewer 'uman. And they say 'ello. And if ewe say 'ello back they think that means ewe've got all the time and they tell ewe everything ewe need to know about Ireland, and everything ewe don't. Did ewe know the surest way to get a sow into a trailer is to try and keep 'er out if it! Only curiosity will get 'er in there ewe see. Anyway, put the kettle on, will ewe? I'm gagging."

Harris was standing in the middle of the room, next to the tree trunk that held the roof up, and was looking around.

"Ewe do 'ave a kettle, do ewe?"

Ed was standing by the open front door. He was scratching his head. Something was wrong. More wrong than the fact that Harris was not in Wales.

Ed looked at Harris's feet. And he knew what was wrong. Not since Cat was born on the beach had Ed seen Harris without Cat.

The poor man was hurting. Hurting bad.

It took two pots of tea to tell the story. Cat had got sick, and the vet said he would give her an injection, but Harris told him to fuck off and took her home so he could cure her.

Cat was uncomfortable all right, but the idea of sticking a needle in her and filling her with poison was too much. Harris had given her life; he was not ready to take it away.

The world had better get ready for some supernatural healing. Harris was going to love her better.

Cat could not eat so Harris did not eat. He drank when she drank. He slept when she slept. His boss gave him a week off. Then sacked him because he sat with Cat for the guts of a month until she passed away.

"During that month I realised even Cat 'ad to die. Even a puppy dog that is so destined to live it survives being lobbed into the winter sea in a bin bag, so determined to survive, even that strength must one day succumb...the bitch...Sometimes our breathing and our 'eart beats were synchronised and I sensed 'ow one day I would exhale and not inhale again...it was frightening. And freeing.

"I 'ad never even given much thought to what may be next. That's no way to go through life, is it? It o-curred to me that this life is just one sheet on a never-ending toilet roll. And the beginning is out of sight too. It behoves us to become intimate with the idea of dying. As we get closer to death, if we can become more familiar with what it is and what it isn't we will live lighter, clearer, freer lives. Cat was showing me 'ow it is. All this…" Harris looked around, holding out one hand, touching the air and rubbing his fingers together. "…all this, everything, is just window dressing. From day one she was the most precious gift. It's like Dr Seuss says, *Don't cry because it's over, smile because it 'appened.* Good, init? The lads from The Stars sent me a card with that on it. Why do people wait till something big 'appens before they prove they're 'uman?" And he started crying again.

"I buried Cat between the pools at Aberedw Rocks. We'll go there next time ewe are over." It was a command, not an invitation, which was fine by Ed.

"A good choice for her final resting place – well above sea-level," said Ed, his tone full of respect.

"Do ewe remember the last time we was up there, all three of us together?"

❖

Ed's folks had a caravan on a remote farm the other side of Aberedw Hill. Ray had offered to drop them at the pub, he was going to Builth himself anyway that evening. They could walk back over the hill. It was a clear sky, there would be half a big moon.

During the afternoon they ate Fray Bentos steak and kidney pies with puff pastry that you can cook in the tin. Also boiled potatoes and peas. And tea which they drank out of pint glasses.

Ed was stuffed. He fell asleep on the sofa at the big-end of the caravan while Harris opened a tin of rice pudding, put a

191

large spoon of strawberry jam in it and mixed it in. He gave the first spoon to Cat before quaffing the rest.

When Ed opened his eyes and looked out of the window, he saw great clouds of parachutes falling out of the sky.

Harris put down his guitar and came over for a look.

"'Er Majesty's Army," he said.

At five o'clock they went to find Ray and his wife Ruby. They were standing in the field looking at…they were looking at…the field.

"What are ewe looking at?" asked Harris.

"Nature, my boy, nature," said Ray. People who called Harris *my boy* would usually receive a good kicking. Ray had lived on this farm all his life; it had been in the family for generations. It was impossible to say where the farm ended and Ray began. And vice versa.

They walked down to the yard. "First time those chicks have been from the shed, they were only out the eggs last Sunday. But they knows their job, look, straight into the grass…"

Mother was leading the brood towards the stream. "That's going to be cold for 'em. Still they ain't got long, we'll have the heads of 'em a day or two after December the twelfth."

Ed had returned from Nepal a vegetarian but hearing that did not disturb him. They were on Ray's farm. And Ray had said it. Cat got the vibe too and was on Harris's heel the whole time. Not out of subjugation. She was showing off. I know how to behave. I am a professional too.

Harris squeezed into the back seat, leaving no space for Ed. He got in anyway, and the front passenger seat tipped back on him. Ruby sat on that, and Ray steered them down the lane to the road.

He drove slowly. Ray and Ruby looked in every field, hedge, tree, missing nothing. It was their TV. Driving to Builth was their soap opera.

"See 'em? On the rise…"

"Little 'uns."

"Three, no four."

Ed looked out the window, not a clue what they were seeing.

Ray and Ruby got the news by listening to the radio a lot, and the postman would often stop for a cup tea. A car would not pass the end of the lane without them noticing, and from the sound of the engine and the time of the day they'd probably know who was driving.

They had a sixth sense about the animals, and if anything else happened, like a cloud of parachutes dropping one afternoon, well they'd know, of course.

"Probably SAS. You never hear a plane, you just see 'em dropping then they are gone. In February we were told there were 120 of them on exercise in this area, two weeks they were about and no-one saw nothing – plenty of snow on the ground too."

Ed waited for some mind-blowing exception, how Ray and Ruby found them out. Maybe Ray noticed the owl was acting differently and found a squaddie sheltering in the roof of their barn or…

"No-one saw nothing?" he asked finally having to elicit the required end-of-the-story.

"That's right. Nothing," said Ruby matter of factly.

In the pub Harris was happy and inspired. He asked Ed if he knew you could estimate the age of a hawthorn hedge by allowing about a century for each plant species established in it. Ed said that he did not.

"Actually I have been thinking about the walk home and the fact that there is a battalion of killing machines camped out between us and where we need to go."

"Me too," said Harris, signalling for two more beers. "And I like our chances. We'll 'ave the advantage of surprise – it'll be after midnight, there'll never expect an assault from this direction. And we'll be pissed. Nice and relaxed, we'll feel nothing. After that they 'ave all the advantage."

After a few moments of a shocked Ed, Harris looked at him and smiled as if to say, "I'm only joking", but it was a corner-of-the-mouth smile, unconvincing.

They climbed the gate, their eyes already well adjusted to darkness. The path wound up the hill in front of them. A world of dark silhouettes and shadows. Ed's agile, untrained mind had been fed eight pints of Thumpton's Special and was easy prey for doubt and fear.

That was before Harris lit the spliff. In the fresh air after a gallon of beer it was a real pleasure to inhale the hot smoke. Harris gave Cat a blowback. She stopped yapping and started running in circles under their feet.

Ed stopped for a piss. "Here, Harris, come here. Just wondering...how old would you say this hedge is?"

Harris pushed Ed. Not very hard. It didn't have to be. It took Ed a while to get the hair out of his eyes, figure out which way was up and find his way out of the hedge, by which time he'd finished weeing.

It was a still evening, hardly a breath of wind, so the taunts and jibes that Harris shouted carried for at least a mile. It had started with songs but had become a rant.

Ed reasoned that the soldiers would be under orders to stay hidden. Of course that was the whole point of the exercise. At the same time these guys would be wired really tight and the temptation to hood and cuff and interrogate a two-man anti-English protest on the way home from the pub would be considerable, no?

With the right know-how it was possible to beat the shit out of someone without leaving a mark. Everyone knew that.

Near the top of the hill they had a choice: there was a hundred metres of jumping from one tuft of bog-grass to the next, or go the long way round, past Twm Tobacco's grave. Harris set off on the direct route, leaping from one tuft of grass to the next.

"Oh shit, sorry, Corporal!" said Harris to a mound that had just shifted under his weight. Then all hell broke loose. Harris kicked the mound flat and booted and flailed in attack and self-defence. It looked like he was surrounded.

Ed tore off at a tangent and was quickly up to his knees splashing through the bog.

Harris was shouting at him, laughing. Laughing?

"Oi!…only joking. Oi!…Lucky I didn't really need any 'elp. Ewe can 'urdle like Colin Jackson when ewe get going, can't ewe?" Then more laughing.

❖

"Yes, don't cry because it's over, smile because it 'appened," said Harris, sobbing hard.

He couldn't stop crying, which was maybe the real reason he left Wales, but he seemed well. He smiled too. Cat's passing had made him look deeply into himself. He had this air about him that anything was possible. And imminent.

"Funny…" said Harris, "when Cat was a puppy, in those first few months she shat and puked all over my 'ouse – combination of being mostly drowned and the 'jections the vet was giving 'er – I'd come down the stairs and catch 'er shittin' or slip in it with bare feet and I'd be fumin' – ready to drop-kick 'er into next week I'd be – and she'd look at me and all my anger in such a way that I saw it myself. She was the victim, why am I mad? And all that red 'ot upset melted. There. In that moment. It's a powerful experience. There's only love then. When all the nonsense falls away, there's only love.

"And when I got the 'ang of it, she stopped doing it. Just like that. Bitch. Like it was all for my benefit, anyway. Then she just found other ways to make me demented." He started sobbing again.

♦

There was a gale off the Atlantic that was sending the waterfalls back up the cliffs. And the ocean froth from breaking waves was travelling two or even three fields inland. The locals were sure it wasn't going to get bad though.

Harris was acclimatising.

"'Tis blowy out. I saw they lash their caravans and garden sheds to the ground, I thought it was to stop 'em getting robbed."

He found Streaky's copy of *The Tibetan Book of Living and Dying* and read the first three chapters three times. "When do I get to meet this Streaky then, anyway?"

"He won't be around."

"Right, I get it. Got so lonely ewe've been making up friends, is it? I knew it! It all sounds too much like a figment of ewer fucked up imagination! Scrambled Ed and Streaky Bacon. Ewer whole life has been so self-indulgent. Sometimes I thought ewer a waste of good oxygen – especially recently. But I shouldn't really judge, I suppose it's what 'appens next that's important.

"It's ironic though. Ewe 'ave spent all these years trying to out run ewer demons, only to come 'ere and act-chew-ally run out ewer demons. The running, and the contemplating ewer navel, 'as definitely improved ewer chances of becoming a responsible 'uman being with something to offer the world. Maybe solitude is not the selfish waste of time that it looks. Depends on ewer motivation really I s'pose, depends if ewer running away from ewer problems, or addressing 'em. Act-chew-ally...maybe it's like the air stewardess was saying before we took off – put on ewer own oxygen mask first. Maybe we need to take a good old toke on clear, clean reality before we can see clearly and try to 'elp others."

"If my old Nanna was still around she'd say ewer a severe case of *hiraeth*. I remember 'er sitting in front of the fire, rocking on 'er chair, smoking 'er pipe, and getting all angsty trying to translate it for me. 'Hiraeth', she said, 'hiraeth is like the beautiful pattern on this rug...' She was tapping 'er 'eel on the 'and woven 'arth rug. Then she flipped the corner of the rug over with 'er foot so I could see all the knots and tangles on the underside. '...And if ewe try to translate it into English, that's what it becomes.'

"Still, Nanna 'ated the idea of 'er favourite grandson growing up ignorant so she 'ad a go at 'aving me understand. She fixed me with 'er bloodshot eyes, saying, 'These days people are scattered, lost, adrift from what really matters. *Hiraeth* names that. It's that longing, the yearning we feel to come 'ome. It's much more than 'omesickness – that word is too common and too weak. *Hiraeth* is not missing ewer mammy! In fact, it's nothing to do with a nostalgia for something we 'ave known in this life, it's more a requirement we feel to take our place in the great scheme of things.'

"Everyone said my Nanna was as mad as a 'at stand but that makes a lot of sense don't it? It certainly sums ewe up."

❖

Harris was looking out on the vast expanse, lost in the view.

"On a good day you can see Wales from here." said Ed

Harris was not well travelled but he knew he was on the West coast of Ireland looking at the Atlantic, next stop America. His head tipped to one side. "'Ow the..."

"...and dolphins too!" said Ed, making sure he was out of thumping range.

❖

Harris looks at Ed's sandals

"Pete Seeger said, *A machine can do it cheaper, an expert can do it better, but I am just going to try and do it myself.* And fair play, boyo, I am not sure ewe could get any cheaper or better."

"It cost me a few cold beers and I got an expert to help me," confessed Ed. He commented on Harris's trainers.

197

"Yep. They are brand new *Nine-Ninety-Nines* – the same as my old ones except they are new. My old ones done about five years. Crackin' pair of runners they were. Miles and miles we done. Along the canal path, over the beaches, through the wood, under the motorway, along the railway – they was more glue than shoe by the end. I'm not one for spending a week's wages on a pair of shoes, I gets 'em down the market. I give 'im a tenner, 'ee gives me a pair of shoes and penny change. Sweet!

"In-varia-bly what ewe need is right in front of ewe, what ewe want is always out of reach. And…"

There was a big pause, a very big pause. Harris's eyes had gone glassy, like someone had turned him off, then suddenly he came back to life.

"…And I have been trialling a theory that our messengers are amongst us, or that wisdom is 'ere if only we could see and 'ear it. I am not talking ghosts or angels, but ordinary, everyday stuff. Like as if nothing was random. Imagine if nothing was random. It's forcing me to pay more attention. In fact sometimes I 'ave to turn it off cause I'm in danger of disappearing up my own crack."

◆

The sun was rising behind a mask of cloud that went crimson, and made the mountain blush too, and the night's rain fell down the rock and crossed noisily under the road. They were on the Healy Pass, an old road that was built for horses and carts so it flowed with the land, from sea-level to 300m in 6km

Coming down the other side they went around the Lough and home over Maulin.

"Cat and me did love all-day adventures. These days people live like caged animals, ewe see. But with regular fresh air'n'exercise she stopped chewing the bottom off doors and I stopped chewing out people and situations – gradually like. It's a process. None of us is perfect immediately. The 'ill-walking 'elps me mind my mind. I worked out a way. It's like a 'ouse party, right. What to do with gatecrashers? They are there, no-one invited them, no-one wants 'em, but kicking 'em out doesn't work, they just come back with their friends…so ewe just leave the doors open, don't offer to 'ang up their coats, ignore 'em and they'll disappear the same way they arrived. That's 'ow I leaves my mind. Neat, init?"

At home they had breakfast even though it was the afternoon. Porridge and a fruit salad with toasted sunflower seeds. And a big stack of American pancakes and maple syrup and rashers and sausages and tea out of pint glasses.

Harris was leaving the next day so they had to make the most of the time. They lit a fire and did nothing.

Harris gave an update on his world tour plans. After Ireland he'd return to Wales and take it from there.

"Ewe said every country is different. Well I like Wales. If I like Wales why would I go somewhere different? And anyway, I gotta get back to start the new job and we 'ave to find a place to live."

"What was that?" asked Ed.

"I like Wales, I'm starting the job – at the dog shelter."

"No, I know, after that. What you said after that, *we* have to find a place to live. *We?*"

" Me and Tiffany. She's my girlfriend."

"Tiffany? Tiffany! What part of Wales does she come from?"

"Bark-shire."

"Berkshire! Berkshire, England! You are going out with, no, correction, you are moving in with, a girl from Berkshire which is in England?"

"'Er granpa was Welsh."

"Jeez, Harris. I blame Cat. I am writing to the Pope. That dog has to be canonised."

Harris sighed out of happiness, but also because it was a huge relief to have made this confession. Not to Ed, to himself.

He'd come out. He was heterosexual with an English girl. And that was okay.

"She was another bonus of 'anging out at the dog shelter, that's where we met, ewe see. I think when Cat saw us together she knew I'd be alright... We're taking it slow. We 'ave to... that's why I am 'ere, y'know, give 'er a bit of space... she's gone back 'ome to break the news to 'er folks. Seems 'er old man is a bit difficult, ee's got a thing about the Welsh. Takes all sorts!" Harris was smiling. He was in a dream, all loved-up and fluffy.

"I tell ewe, boyo – Tiff's gorgeous!"

Ed was in shock. Anything was possible now.

"Ewe know what, Tiff was trying to explain to me what the Buddhists mean when they say 'love is free from attachment'. She explained it out, 'ow what the dogs at the shelter 'ad taught 'er what love is.

"So many dogs come and go, ewe see. Often they arrive in a right mess, and ewe nurse 'em back to 'ealth and ewe just get 'em looking all pretty and strong again and, if ewer lucky, another family comes along and wants to take 'em 'ome. Ewe 'ave to say goodbye. Just like that.

"Love, Tiff said, is not *to 'ave and to 'old* like they tell ewe at weddings. Love is not 'olding on to 'em for dear life, like ewer life depended on it. Cos it don't. No-one needs that kind of love. That's oppression, not love. Love is wishing them, needing them, to be 'appy. Whatever it takes. With ewe or without ewe, 'ere or there. In that way ewer setting them free. And when love is given like that they usually love ewe back. That's a 'ealthy relationship, a love that lasts. I'm just assuming that ewe are still single – that ewer extraordinary por-pensity for failing in relationships has not changed..."

"Yep, still single, but I've had an insight in that direction which is, if you don't even respect yourself how can you respect another. And how attractive is that?"

"That's a cop out!"

"Can it be a cop out and still be true?"

"I guess."

"Okay. Then so it is."

❖

Harris slid the cover back over the engine.

"I always said that camper vans are like speedboats. There are just two memorable days – the day ewe buy it, and the day ewe sell it. The rest of the time they are more 'assle than they're worth. But Mr B is as tidy as they come."

❖

Ed took Harris to Bloc Mór. He told him about kite meditation again.

"How it works is…"

"I get it, Scrambles, I get it. Ewe can 'ave a whole fleet of fancy cars parked in the garage but ewe can only drive one at a time. It's like that with ewer mind. Right?"

10

FLIGHT OF A SOUL ATHLETE

THERE are times when none of it makes sense, the dark wet wild days of winter when you wouldn't put a milk bottle outside the back door. On these days the runner looks at their passion without passion. But they do it anyway.

Then comes the day close to the daffodils and you remember you are sane and there is sanity and all the footwork was worth it. Tenfold.

❧

Ed was on a bit of a high. Sitting on a cliff-top, indigo ocean, clear skies, steady breeze...He has freedom and advantage and he is going to use it.

He is looking at the yacht and looking for jealousy. Oh... there is none! Delighted. Is that pride?

Just feeling their pleasure. And pain.

The pleasure is obvious – it's the perfect sailing day. When you buy your yacht you are dreaming of a day like this, days like this are why you needed to buy the yacht in the first place. So when the day arrives, and you are on your yacht, everything is according to plan. As if you control it. As if you made it happen. As if you are the daddy.

Today is the perfect day. All the circumstances synchronised. The benchmark that captain and crew will measure everything against. Forever. The rest of this life is filled with days dreaming of, and trying to emulate, the one perfect day.

Will the people and the weather and the boat and all the

other circumstances ever conspire in such a favourable way ever again?…

The yacht is much closer now, the sound travels clearly over the surface of the ocean and up to the wall of rock to where he is sitting. He can hear the daddy.

"Sit there, and get your sister to sit there with you, and I don't want to hear another word out of you, otherwise we are turning round…"

"But daaaaad!"

"Right…Ready about!"

Witnessing this he felt a visceral compassionate response which would be unbearable if he felt helpless to help. But he sincerely repeated the simple phrase of loving kindness to them, including all boat-owners past, present and future;

"May you be happy. May you be well." Who knows if it really helped them, but it opened his heart and mind.

He looked down at his muddy feet, and wiped the sweat from his brow, and realised he had a lot of love and happiness to give. And giving it does not make him impoverished or vulnerable, it empowers him.

It's not a finite amount, not a ration queue, its a wellspring, take what you can, share the rest. The more heartfelt this wish is – that these people, his people, have happiness – the better he feels. Streaky had turned Ed onto William Blake. Some lines came to mind.

He who binds himself to a joy, does the winged life destroy.
He who kisses the joy as it flies, lives in eternity's sunrise.

Mind-stoppingly good.

If he had this understanding – kissing the joy as it flies, recognising the illusory nature of all things – in real-time, live, as-it-happens – he would not be dragging the highs and lows of his life behind him like an anchor. They could be wind in his sails.

Nothing was new, yet everything was different. *It had all been with him since the beginning.* But obscured, and in the wrong order. Scrambled.

He looked over his shoulder, at the path rising up in a steady grind all the way to the top, which was out of sight. He wanted to run the hill. The urge to feel the ground, harmonise his cadence to the incline and balance it all out with the arms and with the breathing, the earth, the seagulls and sky.

His body was born to run, he knew that now. But where that had brought him, what was more exciting, was the feeling that his spirit was ready to fly.

"Look at me – not so long ago I needed to jump off a bridge to feel alive, now it's enough just to have some dirt between my toes. Long way to go, but long way travelled."

Right there, right then, there was a feeling of completeness. All his pasts and all his futures were impeccably contained in that present moment. Nowhere to go, nothing to do.

Without leaving that place he got up and ran off.

ACKNOWLEDGMENTS

Sogyal Rinpoche (www.sogyalrinpoche.org) and "The Tibetan Book of Living and Dying" has been the keystone of my life since 1995. I pray that one day I will be able to embody the message it contains. May this book, in some small way, compliment Rinpoche's great faith tradition. May my good intention for writing hugely outweigh any misunderstandings and confusion it may create!

Other significant references for *Running Contra Diction* are: *Running and Being* by George Sheehan (Simon & Schuster, 1978), *Running Wild* by Gordon Pirie (The Sportsman's Book Club, 1962), *Born To Run* by Christopher McDougall (Profile Books, 2010), *Sweeney Astray* by Seamus Heaney (Faber & Faber, 2001), *Kum Nye Relaxation – Parts 1&2* by Tarthang Tulku (*Dharma Publishing, 1978*), *The Berehaven Copper Mines* by RA Williams (The Northern Mine Research Society, Sheffield, UK, 1990), *Everest – Summit of Achievement* by Steven Venables (The Book People Ltd, 2003), *The Drovers' Roads of Wales* by Fay Goodwin and Shirley Toulosn (Wildwood House Ltd, 1977).

There have been so many *influences* of every kind, too many to name, some obviously helpful and others that needed time to reveal their value.

One area of constant support and inspiration are the people of Beara, especially the communities of Dzogchen Beara, Allihies, Castletownbere and Bere Island who helped make the journey what it is.

Aspects of *Running Contra Diction* were formed around enjoyable conversations with Deirdre (and Liza her wonderdog), Tom Cornish, Lisa Downey, Mary Madison, Fachtna O'Donovan, Micheál Ó Coisdealbha, Martin van den Berg, Paul O'Shea, Ella Harrington, Andrew Warr, Dorothy Brophy, Matteo Pistono, Sr Margaret, also Peter, Maura and Helena Murphy – amongst many others... Much appreciation! And *Ola!* to the troop at LUNA sandals for sponsoring the road "shoes", and to Orlagh for the coffee in Cork and a corking cover.

Thanks a million to the gallant readers; Con Hurley, Jackie Keogh, Mary Padwick and Sophia Bigwood.

I never understood why authors harp on about their editors so much ("I mean, did you write it, or did the editor do everything?"). Then I met Maurice and understood what all the fuss was about. In bringing the best out of me and the writing, he has become a most valued mentor and friend. There is a little paragraph in this book that says something like *all you need is one other* Yes *to drown out a world of* No's. Well, that is my humble tribute, Maurice Sweeney.

To my brothers and the boys'n'girls back home, I give you Harris! Thanks for the inspiration. Last and never least, to my wife, our parents and our daughter, who have always been my gravity and the blue sky according to what is required.

Matt Padwick, Beara, February 2015

42946244R00132

Made in the USA
Charleston, SC
12 June 2015